ZOMPOC SURVIVOR:

EXODUS

BEN REEDER

Zompoc Survivor: Exodus

Copyright © 2014 Ben Reeder

Cover design by Angela Gulick| Angela Gulick Design | www.angelagulickdesign.com

Other books by this author:

The Zompoc Survivor Series:
Zompoc Survivor: Exodus
Zompoc Survivor: Inferno
Zompoc Survivor: Odyssey

The Demon's Apprentice series:
The Demon's Apprentice
Page of Swords
Vision Quest (Fall 2015)

Other books available from Irrational Worlds:
The Wormwood Event (Free)

The Dossiers of Asset 108
Rationality Zero
The Primary Protocol

Table of Contents:

Acknowledgements

This book came about largely because of a casual comment from my long-time friend DA Roberts, who told me I ought to write a zombie story of my own. Thanks, DA. I took your advice. Also, thanks for helping me make sure I got the law enforcement and military stuff right. Any mistakes there are mine entirely.

Of course, no book that I write is ever done without the love and support of the love of my life, Randi. I couldn't have done this without your indulgence, your endless patience and your sympathetic ear. You gave me the core of Maya. Even a zombie apocalypse couldn't keep me from you.

Special thanks goes out to fellow writer Tony Baker as well, for pointing some damn fine beta readers my way. Linda Tooch, who went over it with a fine tooth comb in record time, Lee Close and Joel Obertance for your technical input, and Julie Brown for reminding me what my focus was with this project. Because of you, Zompoc: Exodus is much better than it was when you first got it.

To the great guys over at Zombie Tools, thank you for your blessing in letting me use your awesome blades by name. Most importantly, thanks for making such great swords and knives. I'd trust the lives of any of my characters to your craftsmanship…and mine, too.

Be sure to check out the websites listed at the end of the book as well.

Dave's Rules of Survival

1. 98% of survival is mental. Attitude, knowledge and planning ahead will keep you alive when shit hits the fan.
2. Only 2% of survival is physical, but it's an important 2%.
3. Rule of three: 3 minutes without air, 3 hours without shelter, 3 days without water, 3 weeks without food.
4. Plan ahead.
5. Always have a back up for everything. Have a Plan B, because Plan A almost never works.
6. Keep the basics for survival with you at all times.
7. Know your terrain.
8. Always carry a sharp knife.
9. Always know where the exits are and know how to get to them in a hurry and in the dark.
10. Always make sure you know where your clothes and your gear are, and be able to get to them in the dark.
11. Have at least two sources of light at all times.
12. Assume that people suck after shit hits the fan, and that they're after your stuff.
13. Don't be one of the people who suck after shit hits the fan.
14. Guns are not magic wands. If you point one at someone, don't assume they're going to automatically do what you tell them to. Be ready to pull the trigger if they don't.
15. Assume every gun is loaded if you're not in a fight. Don't point a gun at anything you want to keep.
16. Don't count on any gun you might pick up during a fight. There might be a very good reason it's on the ground.
17. Never put your finger on the trigger until you're ready to pull it. Be sure of your target and what's behind it if you do.
18. Know how shit works.
19. Never assume you know enough. Assume you always need to learn more.
20. If shit hasn't hit the fan, it isn't too late to prepare.
21. Always try your plan and gear out before you rely on it to keep you alive.
22. Watch out for your friends and family. No part of your survival prep is more important.

Chapter 1

Terrible Knowledge

No one is so brave that he is not disturbed by something unexpected.

~ Julius Ceasar ~

The zombie apocalypse occurred right on schedule. Some of the dead walked, but most of them drove, all trying to feed their incessant hunger. These zombies weren't trying to eat brains, though. No one ran in fear, and, much to my personal disappointment, no one started shooting the shambling hordes en masse. People just called it Monday and joined their ranks. This was normal, and I walked among them.

For me, the beginning of my Monday came at a more reasonable time: noon. My shift at Provident-American Bank's credit card customer service call center started at one-thirty in the afternoon. And, of course, I was running late. With my car in the shop, my girlfriend Maya was giving me a ride to work. My reflection in the passenger side rearview mirror showed a slightly disheveled man with shoulder length brown hair and dark stubble on his slightly pointed chin. I wasn't exactly model material, not with hazel eyes that were a little too close together and deep set, but Maya thought I was hot. I tucked my green Polo shirt into the waistband of my khaki cargo pants as the big gray building loomed into sight ahead of us. Maya drove up to the entry gate as fast as she could safely, and I handed her my ID badge to wave at the little sensor box. It beeped, and she handed it back to me as she gunned the engine on her little Cavalier and sent the vehicle under the rising bar. The roadway up to the rear entrance rolled past, and she braked to a hard stop in front of the doors as the blue numbers on her dashboard clock changed to read "1:29". I leaned across and gave her a kiss before grabbing my backpack and sliding out of the passenger seat.

"I love you, baby," I said as I closed the door.

"Love you, too. Have a good day. I'll see you tonight!" she smiled at me through the open passenger side window before she drove off. No matter how late I was, I always made time for that. My loafers slapped against the concrete as I bounded to the glass doors and pulled the middle set open to get into the vestibule. It took me three steps to cross to the inner doors and swipe my ID badge against the little black box on the wall, then I was inside the massive lobby and jogging past the pair of blank eyed security guards. Instead of waiting for the elevator, I took the stairs to the second floor and headed through cubicle country to my own personal slice of drudgery. Already the murmur of voices was threatening to lull me into a trance. For the moment, my primary goal was to make it to my cubicle without being seen by a manager. As I slid into my chair and dropped my backpack next to the cubicle wall, I thought I'd made it.

"Hi, Dave. I noticed you were running a little late. Is everything alright?" a cheerful voice came from over my right shoulder as I was logging myself into my station. I gave a silent plea to whatever cubicle gods there might be for patience and stopped entering my password, then turned to face my tormentor. Carol Naismith wasn't even my manager, but she still had the power to make my life difficult. In the rigid environment at P-A Bank, ignoring a manager was considered insubordination, which could mean disciplinary action. Carol was one of that special breed that delighted in using the rules to disadvantage those she felt had an attitude problem. For some reason, the more I tried to toe the line with her, the more certain she was that I had an attitude and needed to be reminded of the error of my ways.

"Everything is fine, Carol. I need to finish logging in so I'm not late." I turned back to my keyboard and waited for her to move on, but she stayed planted where she was. Until she stopped shoulder surfing, I couldn't enter any passwords, which left me stuck between security protocols, which I took seriously, and Carol, who didn't think I took her seriously enough. If I ignored her, she'd write me up for a security violation. If I waited for her to go away, I would end up being late, reinforcing her need to lecture me on the importance of time management even as she prevented me from doing what she was telling me I wasn't doing. Insanity in action.

"I just noticed that you've arrived after your shift starts twice this quarter. What can I do to help you make it to work on time?" Her voice dripped with solicitous concern, every word straight from the manager's playbook. My lips pressed together in a thin line as I fought back the biting remark that was fighting to escape. After a couple of years of corporate double-talk, I was fluent in bullshit, but speaking it still left a bad taste in my mouth. Still, it was the *lingua franca,* as it were, and I had to use it to keep my job.

"As long as I'm logged on within five minutes after my shift starts, I'm on time, Carol. But as long as you're standing behind me, I'm not supposed to enter my password. So, the biggest thing you can do to help me be on time is to let me finish logging in."

"My job is to help you improve," Carol started. She stopped as I stood up and faced her.

"Carol if we're going to have this conversation right now, I need to either let Sue know so she can code me out for the time, or have you do it and *you* tell her why you're keeping me off the phone." I said it all with a smile that promised she wasn't going to like either option. Dropping my manager's name into the conversation changed the tone completely. I didn't always like how my boss did things, and she was as demanding as they came, but when it came to other people interfering with her team getting the job done, she and I saw eye to eye. Carol's smile didn't falter a bit, but she shook her head slightly and took a step back.

"I'll see if I can schedule you some OTP time a little later on and we can have a one-to-one meeting. Go ahead and get on the phone. Our customers need you," she finished with a smile that wouldn't have melted butter. It only took me a couple of minutes to finish logging on to my workstation.

"Way to shut Carol down," Porsche said quietly from her cubicle across the aisle. She had one of those voices that reminded me of smoky rooms and slow jazz. Barely past drinking age, she was more willowy than skinny, and just fashionable enough to avoid being trendy. I turned my head to give her a lopsided grin. Brown hair and bangs that she could have stolen from Bettie Page framed her face as she leaned out in her chair to flash her infectious smile at me. Today, she had on a long tunic in blue with a wide belt around her waist and thin stretch pants in gray. She wore a pair of flat-soled ankle boots that zipped up the side.

"Yeah, I wish I could take the credit for that," I said. A cough broke the gentle chatter of other reps. "How's our call volume today?"

"Pretty slow," she said. She sounded a little surprised, and for good reason. A lot of people thought we were closed during the weekend, so if they had a problem, they waited until Monday to swamp us with calls about how we'd ruined their weekend instead of letting us fix the problem right then. It was a pet peeve of mine, and one of the reasons I disliked Mondays. I finished getting myself set up to take calls and plugged my headset into the phone. It was time to make the donuts.

The first couple of hours were filled with a combination of mind-numbing boredom broken up by inane idiocy. Most of our calls were pretty basic stuff, people calling in with questions about charges they didn't recognize on their bill, disputes with merchants and the occasional plea for us to take a fee off their bill. Most times, we could help them and all was right with their world. Then, there were the idiots. People who didn't think they should pay for the ton of perks their cards gave them, or who thought we were ripping them off because they couldn't grasp how compound interest worked. And as if my day weren't filled with enough Monday goodness, I ended up my first two hours with a call from a guy who threatened to have me fired if I didn't get him a card design in gray instead of blue so it matched all the other cards in his wallet. It was the kind of first world whining that made me sympathize with homicidal maniacs and serial killers sometimes.

When break time rolled around, I grabbed my phone and headed for one of the unused conference rooms in the middle of the building. It gave me the dual advantage of being away from the mass of cubicles and in one of the few quiet places where I had a view of the outside world. I had two texts waiting. The first one was from a phone number with a 307 area code, the sole area code for the entire state of Wyoming. I only knew one person who lived there voluntarily: Nate Reid. He was a former Delta Force operator, and the man scared me the way reading HP Lovecraft's stories alone on a dark and stormy night did. Talking to him was like listening to the audio version of the Necronomicon: something that came out of his mouth was bound to fall into the category of "things mortal men were not meant to know." A year ago, he'd opened my eyes to some of the scariest shit I'd ever heard, and ever since then I'd felt like I was one of those bit players in a spy novel the dashing lead characters consults for important bits of information but who's never in any danger of doing something cool. His text was short and to the point: *Call me. Re: Zoroaster.* I shivered for a second at the code word at the end and checked the next message. It was from Maya.

Going to Mother Murphy's. Want anything? it read. I thought for a moment before sending my response. Mother Murphy's was our favorite natural foods store, and I was jealous that she was going without me.

LaraBars, the usual, cashews & jerky spices, I texted her back. With my metaphorical feet as firmly planted in the arid mental soil of normal as I could manage, I went back to Nate's text and called the number.

"This is Nate," he answered cheerfully on the third ring.

"Hey Nate, it's Dave Stewart," I said. "I got your message. What's up?"

"Have you checked the news today?" he asked.

"No, I haven't had time yet."

"Take a look at what's happening on the east and west coasts today. Go as far in either direction as you can."

"Okay," I said dubiously. "Anything I need to be looking for? Is it something for the book?"

"You know how they say no news is good news? Not today. I gotta go. Remember our deal." He hung up. I was left with a lot of questions and very little time to answer them before I was supposed to start dealing with first world problems of the affluent and clueless. There wasn't a line straight enough to get back to my desk. Porsche came back as I pulled up an internet browser and started looking for news on the coasts. CNN was my first choice, since it posted links to local news outlets. I followed a link about a missing girl in Lake Tahoe being found safe, and it came up with the previous day's date.

"Researching your next book?" Porsche asked as I started sifting through the website for something more recent.

"Not exactly," I said. After I hit another link, I turned to her while the page loaded. "Working on a ghost writing project," I said after a few moments.

"I so don't get that," she said as she tucked her cell phone into her purse. "You've got like six books published and this ghost writing thing. Why are you still working here?"

"Don't let the writing career fool you. On my best day, I'm barely a midlist author. P-A pays the bills so I can keep trying to make it as a writer. The books pay for other things I want to do. Okay, this is officially weird," I said as the page popped up. She came across the aisle and looked over my shoulder at the screen.

"What am I looking at?"

"Notice anything odd?" She shook her head. "Look at the dates. Notice anything out of the ordinary?"

"Everything looks like it's from yesterday," she said after she looked at the list. "What is the page?"

"Breaking news for Channel Nine in Lake Tahoe." She stared at me as I switched to the screen I'd had up before. "And this is for Channel Seven in San Diego. Nothing fresher than Friday. And then for L.A., I got this," I said as I pulled the last

12

page up. The screen showed the news station's logo and banners, but the content showed "Sorry, this page no longer exists."

"That is weird," she admitted. "Wonder what's going on?" I shrugged and gave her a noncommittal sound. She went back to her desk and we both logged back in to take calls. Now that I knew something odd was going on, I started checking peoples' addresses when they called in. The first three were in Iowa, Colorado and Oklahoma. Then I hit paydirt. The address that came up on the account was for Los Angeles, right in the middle of the 90210 zip code.

"How's the weather in L.A. today?" I asked while I was looking through his statement for a set of golf clubs he'd purchased back in July.

"No clue!" he said enthusiastically. "I'm on Seven Mile Beach on Grand Cayman, enjoying rum and reggae. The only reason I'm calling you is because I was supposed to have these damn clubs sent to me here, and now the dealer's saying he never got paid for the god damn things. I need you to help me find out which one of us screwed up!" I assured him that he'd paid the golf club dealer back in July while a feeling of dread crept down my spine. I had no idea why the exception seemed to be proving the theory in my head, but now I was certain that no info was coming out of Los Angeles, San Diego or Lake Tahoe. No calls were coming on from farther west than Colorado, or east of Tennessee. Between calls I went back to checking local TV station and newspaper websites, and kept hitting old news or error pages as far west as Wichita, where the latest update had been posted nearly six hours before. On the one hand, I had to grant that it *was* Wichita. I figured nothing of interest had happened there since Prohibition. But realistically, almost no station or newspaper would go six hours during the day without posting something, even if it wasn't local news. Seeing Wichita going silent worried me more than any major city could. It was only two hundred and fifty miles away from Springfield.

As I sat there and let my brain run through possibility after gruesome possibility, I slowly realized that it had been almost five minutes since I'd taken a call. Heads were starting to pop up over the cubicle walls as people prairie dogged to see if they were the only ones who didn't have calls coming in. Another head popped up and a woman from another team pulled her headset off and headed for the bathrooms. Halfway there, a coughing fit almost doubled her over. Another girl went to help her out as questions flew back and forth about why the calls had slowed down. Of all the people in the room, I was the only one who even had a clue to the answer, and I didn't dare open my mouth about it. No one would believe me. Hell, I barely believed me.

I bet Cassandra had days like this all the time, I thought as I repeated my news search going east. The results in that direction were just as chilling. New York had been silent since Saturday morning, and Washington, D.C. had been off the news radar since Sunday afternoon. So why wasn't anyone else noticing the local news silence? CNN's main feed answered that for me. It was still updating. To my eye, though, the stories it was putting up only reinforced my belief that something was very wrong. All of them were follow up stories that covered things that had happened days ago or stories that weren't time sensitive, what my editor called 'evergreen' pieces. There was no breaking news, just recaps and opinions on stories that were days old. On any other day, I wouldn't have caught that, but today I was hyper-aware of the lack of breaking stories.

If the actual news outlets were off the radar, I was left with one other possibility. Conspiracy websites. I checked the ones I could remember the websites for off the top of my head first. Beyond Top Secret was down, and so was Shadownet. The sites weren't just down; it was as if they had never existed. If anyone else would have spotted the gaps in the news, or even been able to tell the rest of the world what was going on, it would have been the deliberately shadowy figures who ran those sites. There were other sites I could have checked, but not at work, since I didn't have access to the onion router software on the work computers that would have let me get into the darknet, the hidden, anonymous subsurface of the internet.

I stood up and looked out the plate glass window and felt my gut clench at what I saw. Cars were starting to back up on

Highway 60. *No news is not good news,* I remembered Nate's vague warning as I pulled my cell phone out of my drawer. Texting at our desks was frowned upon by the management at Provident, but I figured that pissing off a suit in Maryland wasn't going to be a real serious concern for much longer. Still, I kept the phone under the edge of the desk as I tapped the keys as fast as I could,

No calls incoming. No news from Wich KS & Nash KY, tinfoil hats completely off grid. Noise from the far side of the cubicle farm caught my attention. A Greene County deputy in a gray uniform and one of the security guards in a black blazer flanked the site's on-duty nurse. The deputy looked like he was barely old enough to buy the gun on his belt, much less wear the badge on his chest. I half expected the nurse to introduce him as her son and tell us it was bring your kids to work day.

"I need anyone who's traveled to the following states in the past month to come with me," he said. "Nevada, Arizona, California, Washington, Oregon, New York, Massachusetts or Florida. Anyone who's been to any of those states, come up here now." His voice was just a little too high to take seriously, even when he put his hand on the butt of his pistol. Across the aisle from me, Porsche sank into her chair with a smirk on her face. I dropped back into my chair as a couple of people left their desks. The deputy's face went slack with terror as they got close. It wasn't until the nurse stepped forward to talk to them that he got some of his swagger back.

"I know that guy. He's a total dick," Porsche said. I chuckled at the comment, but my fingers went back to my phone's keypad.

Police just asked for people who traveled to E or W coast. Seconds later, my phone buzzed in my hand.

NE1 sick? Nate's message read.

A few.

Get out. Avoid crowds. Bravo Oscar. My heart nearly stopped when I read the words. I'd been expecting them, but not today. Somehow, I thought I'd have more warning.

Chapter 2

An Ounce of Preparation

A Scout is never taken by surprise; he knows exactly what
to do when anything unexpected happens.~
~Robert Baden-Powell~

During the Korean War, a military term entered the lexicon of civilian use; one used to describe a rapid withdrawal or retreat: bug out. During the Cold War, it had been adopted by survivalists and it had been co-opted by their more modern descendants, the preppers, to describe the exodus from an urban to a more rural location, usually a shelter or safe haven that was stocked up and ready for long term survival.

Bravo Oscar. Bug out.

My mind wrestled with the realization that it was time to get the hell out of Dodge. The more docile part of my brain kept looking for someone else to tell me what to do, for a cooler head to prevail. That was the part that my time at Provident-American had created.

"Alright, everyone, end your calls, log off and let's evacuate to the basement!" my boss was telling us. She rarely emerged from her office unless it was for breaks or to go home, so most days, seeing her away from her desk was a surprise. Today, she had on a pair of black slacks and a sweater over a white turtleneck. Her hair was a bright, coppery color that she kept cut short. It did very little for her looks, but she'd never seemed all that bothered by anyone else's opinions. It was one of the things I respected about her. She led the way toward the elevator, and people just naturally followed her. My corporate brain wanted to, and Porsche was gathering her stuff up to go with her. From across the partitioned jungle, I could see managers and security guards keeping a wary eye on the line of people filing past them.

"My shift is over in a few minutes," one of the guys further down the row said.

"You'll stay here until the sheriff's department gives you the all clear or you're evacuated elsewhere," Deputy Dickhead said as he approached the guy. "If you try to leave before I *say* you can leave, you'll spend the next thirty days in a jail cell. You got that?" He put his index finger in the middle of the man's chest and shoved him back a step. As the guy staggered back, the deputy put his hand on the butt of his pistol again. It was enough to cow the man, but it made me want to slap the officious little prick. Near the entrance to the lobby, I saw a man in a black uniform step into view. He wore a tactical vest that obscured his badge, and a black baseball cap with no markings on it. He looked like a Springfield police officer, but something about him set off little alarms in my head. Nate's advice sounded in my head again.

Get out. Avoid crowds. I grabbed Porsche's arm and gestured for her to cross the aisle. She looked at me in surprise, but she came over. I almost never touched people, and I'd obviously surprised her. I was kind of shocked, myself, but Porsche was as close to a friend as I let myself have at work. I wasn't going to let her follow the masses to their fate.

"Stick with me," I told her as I crouched down in my cubicle.

"Dave, what's going on? What are you doing?" she asked as I grabbed my backpack and pulled the zipper for the main pocket open.

"Saving your ass," I said as I pulled the empty stainless steel bottle out my drawer and dropped it into the bag. She looked at me dubiously for a moment. "I write horror stories. I know when it's a bad idea to do what you're told, and trust me, right now, it's a bad idea. Besides, who do you trust more, me or Deputy Dickhead?"

"You," she replied with a grin.

"Thanks. Grab that soda bottle from your desk, and grab your purse." Mentally, I was cursing my luck on one hand and blessing the name of Nate Reid on the other even as I slipped the pack's single strap across my shoulders. When Porsche came back to my cubicle, I put my finger to my lips for silence, then crouched down and led her into the aisle that ran between our cubicles, heading as far away from the managers as we could get. Once we reached the end of the cubicles, I went to my left, and ended up next to the last row of cookie cutter work spaces. The row of tiny office like spaces ended a couple of feet short of the wall, and I backed into the narrow opening. Porsche slipped in facing me and knelt in front of me. With our faces level with each other, her excited grin lifted my spirits a little.

"Why are we hiding?" she whispered.

"We have to avoid crowds. And for now, we have to stay hidden." She nodded and we waited. The sounds of people faded, until all we could hear was the sound of footsteps pacing between the cubicles.

"Looks like everyone is clear," I heard Sue say.

"Are you sure?" Deputy Dickhead demanded.

"She said they were clear, Deputy," I heard another manager say. I recognized the voice as Chris Jackson. "I think she knows what she's talking about."

"Then get down there with the rest of them, and make sure they don't leave."

"You still haven't told us why we can't let them go home," Sue said, her voice fading.

"You're not cleared to know that, lady. Just do as you're told and let us take care of this," Deputy Dickhead said as the door to the stairwell closed behind them. I peeked over the top of the half wall; the coast was clear, so I nodded to Porsche to move. She backed up and let me out.

"Why do we have to avoid crowds? And what the hell was that all about?" she asked.

"Do you remember my fifth book, Operation Terror? It wasn't all fiction. Neither was The Frankenstein Code." I went into Carol's office and grabbed one of the plastic wrapped promotional fleece blankets she kept under her desk. I tossed it to Porsche then went to the big storage cabinet she kept against

19

the back wall. It was locked, but I knew she kept the key in the second drawer down in her desk. A few seconds was all it took to reveal the snack stash she kept to motivate her team.

"Those horror novels? You've got to be kidding," she said. "That kind of stuff can't happen."

"I hope it can't. I hope we just lost touch with the east and west coast because of a satellite problem or something. But I'm not willing to risk my life on it," I told her as I sorted through the junk food. There were bags of chips, chocolate galore, some hard candy and a few jerky snacks. Some of the chocolate I tossed aside, but the high carb and high protein snacks I tossed into a blue duffel bag with the P-A logo on the side. She also had a selection of energy drinks in the back. I tossed a couple of those in, and uncovered a few juice drinks too. All of those went in the bag. Lastly, I grabbed a couple of t-shirts and a sweat shirt.

"I still don't get it. What does all of that have to do with you looting Carol's office?" Her tone sharpened, and I stopped what I was doing. From her point of view, what I was doing could get us fired. To her the world was still normal. Nothing had changed. I set the duffel bag down on Carol's desk.

"Okay. Here's the deal. In 2006, there was an outbreak in Baqubah, Iraq. The people who were infected with the disease suffered some kind of brain damage that made them *really* aggressive. It almost broke out, but the Army stopped it by killing all of the people who were infected. They thought that was it, but a year or so ago, it popped up again. Only this time, it was in the US. They had to destroy an entire town to stop it that time. I got the inside scoop on it from two guys who were there both times, and I've been able to verify enough to make me believe them." I watched her face to see if she believed me. She frowned, but she wasn't telling me I was full of shit, either.

"I'm still not sure I be…what was that?" she said as she shook her head. The quiet *pop!* that intruded on the quiet had sounded to me like a gun shot. I headed over to the window, and in the fading sunlight, saw a scene straight out of one of my stories. The line of cars was now a mass of people locked in combat. Faint screams reached us even through the thick plate glass. Even as we watched, we saw people racing across the parking lot toward the carnage on the road. A few broke off, and headed for the front doors.

"Oh my God," Porshe whispered. "Who are those people?"

"They're not people anymore," I said somberly. "They're carriers. It's called the Asura virus. It turns people into hyper-aggressive cannibals. Now you see why we have to avoid crowds and sick people." I turned and headed back to Carol's office to grab the duffel bag. Porsche didn't resist when I thrust it into her hands.

"Do you have a safe place to go outside of Springfield?" I asked.

"I could go to my dad's place in Kansas, I guess. It's petty remote," she said shakily.

"Hang on to this. It isn't much, but it's the best I can do for you on short notice for a bug out bag. This stuff might last you for about three days, but if you can supplement it somehow, do it. You still need a map, a knife and shelter."

"What about you?" she asked.

"Dave's survival rule number six: Keep the basics for survival with you at all times. I always have my everyday carry stuff on me, and I have a bug-out bag at home." I unslung my pack and unzipped it to show her the gear I'd been carrying around with me for the past few months. Inside was a kit with a pocket knife, a small penlight and a compass, a box of waterproof matches, a personal first aid kit and an LED flashlight. Adding my sweatshirt, a couple of Frisbees and the metal water bottle to it, and I had all the things I would need for the five mile hike home. Everything, that is, except a gun. Right then, I really wanted a gun. However, I wasn't completely without options in the weapon department.

I led her to the water fountain and filled my water bottle, then dumped the soda out of her bottle and refilled it with water. Once we had that done, I went to one of the coat closets. As she watched from the doorway, I popped one of the heavy bars out of its socket and pulled it free. I did the same on the other side, giving us each a three foot long metal club. It wasn't much as improvised weapons went, but it was better than our fists and harsh language.

"What else do we need to do?" she asked as she hefted her club.

"Well, if you have to go to the bathroom, now would be a good time. Use the men's room, though. The lady who used the other one last didn't look so good." She paled a little at that, and followed me into the men's room. I checked both stalls, then grabbed a paper towel from the dispenser and soaked it in anti-bacterial soap. Once I had wiped down the seat, I gestured her toward the stall with a half-bow.

"I'll be right outside," I said as I moved to the door to give her a little privacy. We traded places after she was done, then headed back into the hallway and toward the windows that looked out over the north side of our wing. A crowd of people had gathered at the door I had come in a few hours ago. The south side was even worse, with people from the highway joining the larger crowd there. The west end of the wing also had a crowd of people pressed up against the door to the smoking area.

"Crap," Porsche said. "What about the east side?"

"Good thinking. There are three entrances on that side. We just need to make sure they're clear before we try to go out." I went to one of the emergency evacuation maps on one of the pillars and broke the plastic cover so I could pull it out. It showed the building as a T shape with the vertical bar pointing to the west, and the cross bar running north-south. We were located at the bottom of the T, as far west as we could be. Most of the infected seemed to be piled up near the junction of the two bars on the west side. The east side only had a narrow parking lot that abutted on the rear of a residential area.

"There's the two entrances on the east side," she said, pointing to them, each one north and south of the vertical bar. "But you can see them from the main doors. What about the north and south entrances at the end of the wings?"

"Maybe, but they're still too close to being visible from the main entrances. There's another exit on the east side, though. Right here," I pointed to a small notch set just north of the T juncture on the east side.

"There is?" she said with surprise in her voice.

"Yeah. Found it last year. Dave's Rule Number Nine: Always know where the exits are and how to get to them in a hurry or in the dark." As I quoted my personal survival rule, I folded the map and put it in the right hand cargo pocket of my pants. Porsche followed me as I headed for the door to the main lobby. She started to go for the stairs to our right when we got there, but checked herself when I kept going straight. The guard desk was abandoned, but the lobby wasn't empty. Deputy Dickhead and one of the guards were standing in front of the south entrance, staring at the mass of people on the other side of the glass doors. The thick security glass would probably hold against the crowd that was there, but I wasn't keen on seeing how much more it could take. I gestured to Porsche for silence, and we slowly crept along the walkway that ran along the north and west sides of the lobby. Deputy Dickhead was talking into his radio, demanding some backup, while the security guy just stood there with his arms hanging at his sides. I stopped when we came to the most exposed part of the balcony, where it crossed over the foyer for the north entrance and became a catwalk for about twenty feet. Below us, I could hear the shuffle of someone's feet. I stopped to take a look at the mass of infected on the other side of the doors. Empty eyes stared at the people on the ground level, and I found myself fighting the urge to just run. When I moved again, some primal urge told me to move even more slowly. It took a full minute to cross the intervening twenty feet to the threshold of the east building, but none of the infected caught sight of us, nor did the men who were supposed to be protecting us. I kept on going until I crossed the open work area and reached the windows that looked out over the narrow east parking lot. There was a large group of infected lurking near the south end of the building, but they were mostly just wandering aimlessly. The north side was almost abandoned. All we needed to do was get to the exit.

"Okay, the exit's clear," I said softly. Relieved, I pulled out my phone. Now that I had a plan, I needed to coordinate with Maya. The blinking light of a waiting message winked at me as I slid the phone open. The preview menu showed Maya's number, and I hit the view option expecting a message asking if I was okay. Instead, the words I read made my insides turn to water.

Chapter 3

Xanatos Speedchess

Adapt or perish, now as ever, is nature's inexorable imperative.

~ H. G. Wells ~

Went in to cover a shift at work for June. Can you get a ride home? Maya's text read. I stifled the urge to curse, but only half succeeded.

"What's wrong?" Porsche asked quietly.

"My girlfriend went in to work," I said.

"Doesn't she work at an old folks' home or something like that?" she asked. I nodded, for some reason glad she'd remembered.

"Yeah, but if you say that to her face she'll hurt you. It's a convalescent and rehab facility."

"Either way, it's crowds and sick people. You better tell her to get the hell out of there." She hadn't even finished the sentence before I was dialing Maya's number. She didn't answer after five rings, and it went to voicemail.

"Baby, it's Dave. You have *got* to get out of there, *now*! I'm headed your way. Text me when you leave." I closed my phone and took a slow, calming breath. There wasn't much I could do from here, so I had to get my focus back on handling my own situation. I still had to get out of the building, and I still had to get to Maya. Only the destination had changed.

"So, what now?" Porsche asked.

"Nothing changes. We get out of here. You head to your dad's place. I go get my girlfriend. Now, we focus on getting you to your car. Where did you park?"

"My truck's on the north side," she said. I nodded and headed for the hallway.

"Yeah, they're just standing outside the doors," we heard from the stairwell ahead of us. "They just keep staring at me. It's creepy." A staticy voice replied, something about not abandoning his post. It didn't surprise me that they'd posted a guard at the side entrances. I pulled up short right before we got to the open stairwell and turned to Porsche.

"We're going to take the stairs up to the third floor," I whispered. "Stay low and don't make a sound." She nodded and followed me as I crept to the walkway that led to the north building. The stairs were right next to the entry, and I slowly crept up the steps to the landing between floors. The part of the building we had just left only had two stories above ground, and the one we were going to had three. A glassed in stairwell connected them. Through a narrow gap between the landing and the top of the glass door, I could see the small group of infected waiting at the outer set of doors to the side entrance. Something about what I was seeing struck me as wrong, and I stopped to take a closer look.

It took me almost a minute to see it. None of the infected were pulling at the handles to the door. For all I knew, the outer doors were still unlocked, and the only thing stopping them was the way the hinges worked. Even dogs could be trained to pull on door handles, and they didn't have opposable thumbs. I slowly shook my head and crept up the next flight of stairs to the walkway that led into the third floor of the north building. I looked around, but no one seemed to be in here either. I'd never heard any part of the center so quiet, and the silence pressed against my ears like something sinister as we crossed the empty floor. The sound of the metal cap of my water bottle seemed too loud in my ears as I unscrewed it and downed a few gulps of water. I heard Porsche curse from the northern windows as I put the cap back on.

"What's wrong?" I asked as I walked over to her. She pointed to a handful of infected wandering among the parked cars.

"There's my truck," she said, indicating a blue light utility truck on the other side of the infected.

"That does change things a little," I said as I looked down at the latest obstacle.

"What are they doing?" she asked. The question took me aback for a moment, since I thought the answer was more than a little obvious. But Porsche was better with people than I was, and it made a kind of sense that I tended to miss. No one did things for no reason, not even brain damaged cannibals. Keeping that in mind, I started to see a pattern in the way they were moving.

"I think they're looking for something," I said slowly. "The question is, what?" A moment or two later, the answer darted out from under a car, on the opposite side from one of the infected. It was a black and white cat, and it moved with the speed of the desperate. It dodged between two of the infected but didn't manage to escape the reach of a third. For a moment, it squirmed as its captor tried to take a bite out of it. Then it got its back legs against his forehead and went sailing away, leaving the confused cannibal with nothing for his efforts but a handful of loose fur. In a blur of black and white, it was under the cars again. The infected lurched around looking for it, but the little ninja feline had learned its lesson well. As the hunters went looking for where they'd last seen it, it rocketed out from under another car several rows down and made for the houses behind the center.

"Thank God!" Porsche gasped as it made the safety of a manicured yard.

"Smart kitty," I said. "Very smart. Okay, I know how we're going to get you to your truck. Grab the cords from a few headsets, and those beanbags over by the toss game. And if you find any of the footballs people throw around, grab a couple of those, too. Anything that you think we could throw."

"Where are you going?" she asked.

"Gonna go open a door," I said as I headed for the stairs. The roof access doors were always locked and only the maintenance team and security had badge access. All I had was a steel bar. Sure, I could bash my way through if I had a few hours, but I didn't. Well, strictly speaking, I had more than a steel bar. I also had Dave's Rule Number Eighteen: Know how shit works. Doors have a few weak points, if you can get to them. One is the hinges. The other is the doorknob. Once I reached the door to the roof, I put myself next to the hinges and raised the bar over my head in a two handed grip, then brought it down as hard as I could on the door handle. The shock of the blow stung my hands, but the handle bent. It broke on the second try and clattered to the ground. My hands slid along the smooth surface of the bar as I changed my grip on it, then I slammed the end of it against the opening where the handle had once been. The other side of the handle popped out on the other side on the first hit, then the rest of the inner workings gave way on the next. With nothing to hold the latch in place, the door swung open with only a little fiddling.

My part done, I headed back to the floor to find Porsche dumping a pair of small footballs into a cardboard box.

"What's all this stuff for?" she asked.

"Distraction," I answered as we headed for the stairs again. The stairway to the roof was musty and hot. Off to our right we could see the access to the elevator machinery, and right in front of us was the doorway to the roof. The door opened easily enough, but I dropped my backpack against the doorjamb to keep it from closing all the way as we stepped out into the fading light of Monday afternoon. The sun was sinking in the west, making the horizon a forbidding red. I walked slowly to the edge of the roof and took a long look at the view.

"This is one of those moments you're going to remember for the rest of your life," I said.

"What?"

"The sun's setting on the world we know. When it comes up tomorrow, it'll be on a new world. For the rest of your life, you're going to look back on this day, and remember where you were when the world ended." She looked at me with a disbelieving frown.

"You're getting philosophical *now*?" she said. I shrugged.

"No, just…aware of the moment. Funny how the game changers are hardly ever pleasant. Okay, moment's done. You ready to hear the rest of my master plan?"

"You have a plan?" she laughed.

"Dave's Rule Number Four: Plan ahead and always have a backup plan. We need to get the infected interested in something else. Plan A is to set off a car alarm and hope they go check it out. Plan B is to get their attention on us up here on the roof, draw them over to this side of the building and then make a break for the other side."

"Do you have a plan C?"

"Nah. Plan B almost always works," I said as I dug through the box of stuff. She'd grabbed a handful of half sized footballs, a good dozen tossable beanbags and about a dozen of the headsets. I pulled one of the headsets out of the box and pulled the detachable end free, leaving me with just the spiral cord and the heavy plug in base. Dangling the heavier end about two feet from my hand, I spun it around a few times then let it go near the top of its arc. The cord streamed along behind it as it flew in a gentle curve away from the building…and tangled up in one of the decorative trees at the end of the row.

"Why don't you start with Plan B then?" Porsche asked.

"Because then it would be Plan A, and thus destined to fail," I said as I hefted one of the beanbags. I hurled it as hard as I could, and it cleared the tree, but when it landed, it barely made a sound and no car alarm went off.

"Don't aim at the crappy cars. Aim for that yellow Mustang over there." The car in question was in the middle of the row I'd landed the beanbag on. "The better looking the car, the more likely it has a car alarm." With her advice fresh on my mind, I grabbed one of the footballs and gave it my best throw. It fell short, and bounced off the hood of a car two spaces before my target. We could hear it hit from the roof, and we saw some of the infected turn that way. Porsche grabbed a football and lobbed it in the same direction. Hers flew in a smooth spiral and hit the roof of the same car mine did, but instead of bouncing off to the side, it did a slow, high arc, hit the roof of the next car, then landed on the hood of the car we were aiming for. The horn started blaring and the headlights went on, and infected started moving toward the noise.

"Whaddya know? Plan A worked! Plan A almost never works. Let's go," I said as I broke into a sprint for the door.

Speed was more important than stealth as we pounded down the stairs. The sound of our footsteps clattered off the walls as the second floor went by, then we were at the ground level, facing the door to the call floor. I popped the door open and took a quick peek. A guard was standing with his face pressed up close to the glass doors about fifty yards from us, with his radio up next to his mouth. Directly across from us was the narrow hallway that led to the emergency exit. I looked over my shoulder at Porsche and she gave me a nod. She pulled the door the rest of the way open, and shrugged her purse and duffel bag over her shoulder.

I darted across the open space and didn't slow down once I was in the hallway. We were ten steps from freedom, but I had to admit to myself that it might get even more dangerous for us the moment we stepped outside the door.

Five steps away, and my doubts grew. Was I really helping Porsche by getting her out of the building, or was I just making sure she died sooner rather than later?

Two steps away, and my hand was almost on the door. Sudden certainty hit me. I knew that there was no question of *if* she would end up infected staying here. It was only a matter of *when*. On the other side of that door, she would have a chance.

My hand hit the bar, and I left doubt at the door. I was giving Porsche control over her own fate; it was the best anyone could do right now. The emergency alarm was shrill behind us as we sprinted for the first row of cars. We ducked down behind a gray minivan as the blaring sound was suddenly muted by the door closing, and made our way between the front grills of two more cars before we were forced to slip out to the second row. My shoulders tensed as we crouch-walked behind the parked

30

cars, feeling extremely exposed. I kept my head moving, looking for infected as we went. Every step felt like I was in a horror movie, and that the audience was screaming at me not to go into the dark room. My nerves were wound as tight as a drum by the time we reached the end of the row. Twenty feet of asphalt separated us from the next row of cars. In my head, I flashed back to being a kid, when the road in front of my house became boiling lava or a piranha infested river. Open space seemed almost as dangerous right now.

"Okay," I breathed. "Last stretch. You ready to make a break for it?" I looked back over my shoulder, but Porsche's brow creased in uncertainty.

"What are you going to do from here?" she asked.

"I'm going to go get my girlfriend," I explained.

"On foot? And then what?"

"Yeah. I know some back ways. And then we're getting the hell out of Dodge. Now, are you ready?" She nodded, and I took off. We stayed low as we crossed the open roadway, then ducked behind the cars. The first fifty yards were fine. The sound of gunshots sounded off to the north as we went, first the crack of single rounds going off, then the harsh hammering of an automatic weapon. More shots came, sounding like a hammer, then a group of short bursts alongside the staccato rip of the other gun. I risked a look over the top of a blue sedan to check on the infected, but their attention was still on the car alarm. Another car alarm went off as one of them stumbled against it, probably drowning out the gunshots. We ran out of cars with six spaces left to Porsche's truck. Another car was parked beside it, and I was guessing it would give us a little cover from the infected that were milling around in front of the building. I turned to Porsche.

"No," she said before I could open my mouth. I gave her a blank look.

"Huh?" I said feeling particularly nonplussed.

"We're not splitting up yet," she said firmly. "There's no way I'm letting you *walk* all the way to wherever your girlfriend is, and I'm sure as hell not going to try to get out of town by myself. So, you're stuck with me. Deal with it." Porsche's stock went up a few points in my book as she gave me a determined look. I gave it half a moment's thought, and realized I didn't even need to do that. Aside from having a cool head on her shoulders, Porsche was another human being. I couldn't just leave her on her own. Right now, I was bound by one of my own rules; one Porsche was following without even knowing it. Besides, this was really not the place to argue the finer points of anything.

"Rule Thirteen: Don't be one of the people who suck when shit hits the fan. Thanks, Porsche. It means a lot to me." The gunshots stopped, and I turned to her with a frown as we heard a single scream in the distance.

"Oh, God," she whispered.

"God's too busy with the dead," I said softly. "We make our own miracles now." She nodded and took off for her little Nissan in a crouch.

Chapter 4

Learning Curve

A discovery is said to be an accident meeting a prepared mind.

~Albert Szent-Gyorgyi ~

I followed Porsche to her truck with a growing sense of dread. In the distance, I could hear occasional gunshots and the wail of a single siren. Horns sounded off to the west of us for a few seconds, but stopped as we got to the door of her little blue Nissan truck. I risked another look over the hood, but the infected were still gathered around the blaring car alarms. Porsche tossed her duffle bag into the truck bed before she unlocked her door and slid in, then reached across and unlocked my door. I crawled in, then pulled it closed behind me as quietly as I could manage.

Now that we were in a relatively safe place, I could take a moment to rework my plans. With a vehicle, I had to figure a different route than I would have taken on foot. A truck was faster, but not as versatile. I went over the routes in my head, and chose one from memory.

"You ready to go?" I asked her.

"God, more than ready," she said in a rush. She started the truck up and pulled out of the parking space, then headed for the back gate at a slow crawl. The bars were down at the gate, which wasn't a huge surprise. When the gate worked, it stayed down to prevent the kids from the high school just north of us from using our parking lot as a shortcut. Porsche rolled her window down as we came up to the gate and put her badge up to the little black square of the card reader. It beeped, but the bar stayed put. She swiped it again, and another beep sounded, but the bar stayed down.

"Gate's closed," a voice came over the intercom. I recognized it as Deputy Dickhead. "The city is under martial law. Anyone outside will be shot on site. Surrender now and —"

The rest was lost as Porsche put the truck in reverse and backed up with a screeching of tires.

"Go right! Go right!" I said franticly. She spun the wheel, shifted into first and sent the truck into a sharp right turn that took us down the blocked off drive to the north. "On the grass, head across the field!" I pointed. She took us off the asphalt and we left the smooth road. The little truck bounced diagonally across the hundred and fifty yard wide green swath between the north end of the parking lot and the road, then caught a microsecond of air when we jumped the curb and found ourselves back on asphalt. I risked a look behind us while she fought to straighten us out, and saw only a couple of infected racing across the field. Just as I was about to turn back around, I saw a dark figure on the roof of the south building, the same place we'd been not long before. I pointed to our left, and she took the turn on to Jefferson fast enough to throw me against the door, then slammed on the brakes as we started around the slight curve. I hoped that would throw them off.

A battle field lay ahead of us. Two Humvees were parked in the middle of Jefferson Street, in front of Kickapoo High School. They were surrounded by bodies, but it looked like the vehicles themselves were abandoned. More chilling was the size of the crowd in front of the high school itself, pressed up against three Humvees parked nose to tail in a rough semi-circle at the main entrance.

"Pull in there and kill the engine," I said, pointing to the parking lot of a little insurance office on our left. She got us into the parking lot and slipped in behind a pair of thick decorative bushes that hid us from easy view to the right and in front before she turned the engine off.

"There must be hundreds of kids in there," she said, reflecting my thoughts.

"And a hundred infected trying to get at them," I grumbled. Off to my right, the pair of infected that had followed us from the parking lot trotted by. They crossed Primrose and headed for the throng at the school. "Make that a hundred and two."

"I don't get it. Where are they all coming from?" Porsche asked.

"My bet is a hospital. Probably Cox South, it's just down the road from here. And it's right by the highway. They get out, they infect other people and those people infect other people and so on."

"There's got to be something we can do," she said.

"Well, we can guess that shooting them only goes so far before you end up as dinner for the rest. They do tend to be easily distracted, though. If we get their attention on us, maybe we can get them to chase us and leave the all-you-can-eat-teen-buffet."

"Once we get them to start chasing us, how do we get them to stop?" Porsche asked.

"We get far enough ahead that we're out of sight. Then, we make a couple of turns. Before we do that, though, I want to check the Humvees for weapons. So, here's the plan. I'm going to go check out the Humvees, grab what I can and come back, then we'll ride in, make ourselves a target and save the day."

"What's Plan B?" she asked with a grin.

"Plan B goes something like 'I scream like a little girl and you come get me.'" She laughed at that and nodded. I took a calming breath and opened the door, then slowly pushed it closed. I was across Primrose before the sheer amount of stupid in my whole plan hit me. There was nothing between me and a hundred infected but a thirty yards of air and ignorance. If they saw me, I only had a few seconds before they were on me and I was just another victim. If they didn't see me, I stood to gain a little extra gear and maybe…just maybe, we could buy the kids at Kickapoo a little more time.

I found myself crouching low as I got closer, even though it probably didn't really help anything. It made me feel better, and I really needed that. I could hear the movement of the crowd of infected with every step. They uttered a low, constant groan that was unnerving even from a distance. I couldn't imagine how nerve-wracking it must have been up close. When I finally made it to the first circle of bodies, though, I had other things on my mind. Most of the bodies were either in patient smocks or scrubs with the Cox logo on them, bearing out my guess. Patients and hospital staff. My brain went straight to the worst case scenario with Maya, and I fought to keep the rising sense of despair from overwhelming me. Until I knew otherwise, I had to keep Maya alive in my head, making it the girlfriend version of Schrödinger's cat.

The dead slowed me down as I tried not to step on them or in the pools of blood they were laying in. Once I made it behind the closest Humvee, I leaned up against it and let myself relax just a little. The smell of cordite and blood filled my nostrils and I decided to spend as little time as I could there.

Despite the ghoulish sound of my original plan, I had an ulterior motive for wanting to check out the Humvees. If the soldiers who had been in them had been overrun, odds were good that no one would ever know what happened to them. Every soldier was issued a pair of dog tags, and I intended to collect the second tag so that someday, I could make sure someone knew what happened to these men. When I'd been in the Air Force, I was required to wear both of mine around my neck, but when I was writing for Nate, I learned that some units wore their second tag laced into their boot instead. I crept up to the first body in BDUs and steeled myself to check the right boot. The shiny metal reflected the fading sunlight. Right the first time. Rather than try to unlace it, I moved up a little and grabbed the combat knife from his belt. The tag came free after a quick slice against the boot lace, and I went to the body lying near the front of the other Humvee. This guy had his in the same place, and I cut it free. Both men had gaping wounds at their necks that made me a little queasy to look at. From where I was, I couldn't see another body, so I went around the front of the lead Humvee to check the other side. Sure enough, I found another body, lying in plain sight of the school.

I moved as quickly as I dared, using the vehicle's shadow to conceal myself as I cut the boot laces to get his tag. As much as I wanted to get behind the Humvee, I forced myself to grab the pistol from his tactical holster and pull the extra magazines from the pouch beside it before I snuck back to the far side. Once I had my back to the driver's side door, I took a quick look at the pistol I'd taken. Survival rule number sixteen was to never trust a gun picked up during a fight, and this was close enough to qualify. You never knew if it was on the ground for a damn good reason. The ubiquitous M9 pistol was one I'd been trained to use back when I was in the Air Force, but I'd never drawn one outside of the target range. I pulled the slide back and chambered a round, then clicked the safety off, keeping my finger outside the trigger guard. That was rule seventeen: never put your finger on the trigger until you're ready to pull it. Now I had fifteen rounds of nine millimeter ammunition to hand. I tucked the two spare magazines into my right hand cargo pocket and went to the nearest body. His pistol was on the ground near him, with the spent magazine still in it. I undid the leg straps and unbuckled his belt. His ammo was in the pouch on his holster, and he had his combat knife on his belt. I fastened the belt again and slung it over my shoulder, then went to his rifle. Even in the twilight, I could tell it was trashed. The collapsible stock had been bent and the magazine well had been crimped. Empty magazines were lying near the front tire, and I only found one in his vest. I tucked it into my cargo pocket as well, and crouch-walked to the first body I'd checked. He still had his pistol holstered, so I repeated the process with his belt and slung it, replacing his combat knife in its sheath, too. His rifle still looked intact, so I grabbed it and checked his ammo pouches. That netted me two more magazines, plus what was left in the one still in the well. I slung his rifle over my shoulder and tucked the two magazines into my bulging cargo pocket. As I crept back to the end of the Humvee, I heard movement inside it.

I jumped when a bandaged hand slapped against the window. Only three fingers showed through the bloody bandages, and it left a red smear on the glass as the man in the Humvee pulled himself into view. His eyes were milky and distant as he stared at me from the other side of the glass. Every part of my brain was trying to tell me to run, but I couldn't take my eyes off of him or even move from the sheer terror. Movement to my left caught my attention a microsecond before a cold hand grabbed my ankle.

I screamed like a little girl. Okay, it was more of a yelp, but it was high pitched and very unmanly. And I so didn't give a fuck who heard me. I yanked my foot free and looked down to see the first soldier reaching for my foot again. I backed up and watched in horror as he slowly climbed to his feet. My body injected adrenaline into my blood in prodigious quantities, and I made the coin flip in my head: fight or run. Oddly enough, fight won, and my left hand came up. The Beretta barked twice in my hand and the guy went down. Behind him, I could see his buddy getting to his feet as well. Some part of me wanted to stare in slack jawed disbelief, but my forebrain was telling me to look for the strings or the man behind the curtain or whatever was making it happen *later*.

The first guy started getting back to his feet. *Ballistic vest,* I thought, and pointed the gun at his face. The gun bucked on my hand and he fell back again. Then I raised my aim to his buddy. My hand was shaking too badly to be sure of the shot, and he kept moving around as he came toward me. I put a round center mass to knock him down, then ran up to him and put a round through his head to be sure. *Five rounds.*

Pale light hit the area, and I could see the rest of the prone figures around me start moving.

"Oh, fuck," I whispered as I realized how deeply screwed I was. Never mind the horde at the school, I had a double dozen infected right *here*! The guy from the other side of the Humvee lumbered into view, and I brought the pistol up. Luck was with me and the round disintegrated the left side of his face. *Six.*

The headlights from Porsche's truck got closer as the dead infected started getting back to their feet. These people had *already* been shot several times each, but the head shot guardsmen seemed to be staying down. I missed the first shot at the forehead of the guy in scrubs closest to me, but the second round took the top of his head off. *Seven, eight.* An older man in a blood drenched smock lurched to his feet off to my left, and a woman in scrubs made it to her knees on my right. Shooting to my weak side first, I managed to hit the woman in the forehead but I missed the guy in the smock the first and second time. The third round hit his left eye and he went down. *Nine, ten, eleven.* Another man got to his feet right in front of me, silhouetted against Porshe's headlights for a split second before she introduced his ass to her truck's front grill. He went flying past me as she skidded to a stop beside me. I took a second to thin the odds by two more before I jumped in the bed of the truck. *Twelve, thirteen.* More of the infected were streaming across the parking lot.

The little window in the back glass slid open as she pulled away. "Are you okay?" she yelled over the wind and engine noise. Behind us, I could see the crowd of infected turning to follow us.

"I'm fine!" I called back as I dropped the magazine out of the Beretta and fished in my cargo pocket for a fresh one. "My boxers are ruined, though. Stay on Jefferson as far as you can, but don't go too fast. The important part of Plan A is working." The new mag slid home and I reset the count in my head. I grabbed the nearly empty magazine from my lap and stuck it in the left side cargo pocket.

"Plan B seemed to go the way you called it!" she said with a nervous laugh.

"Heard that, did you?"

"Oh, yeah. You sounded just like my niece. Except for the shooting." She kept the truck going slow enough that the infected could keep us in sight and follow us. They were surprisingly fast for brain damaged cannibals. They kept up with us as we entered the residential area behind the school and rounded the first curve. It bent to the left, then back to the right, and they followed us through them without losing pace. When we reached the intersection for Walnut Lawn, it looked clear. The stop light was blinking red, but the road was empty. Behind us, the infected weren't showing any signs of slowing down, so I turned back to the window.

"Alright, pick it up once we make it through the intersection," I told her. She ran the blinking red light and hit the gas as we crossed the deserted street. Streetlights lit patches of road, but long stretches were dark as we drove toward Battlefield. Gunshots peppered the silence, and in the distance, I could hear the rhythmic thump of a helicopter's rotors. Off to my left, I heard a single scream pierce the night before it was cut off.

Safe for the moment, I unslung the assault rifle and the two pistol belts, then pulled my backpack off and dug my sweatshirt out for a little protection from the chill in the October air. With it on, I stood up and leaned against the back of the cab. The cool air blew through my hair and I took a moment to process what I'd learned. Shooting the infected wasn't enough to stop them. Only headshots put them down for good, and even that was a maybe. Even more frightening, I had watched dead men get back up and move. Diseases weren't supposed to affect dead people. I considered and rejected the idea that they weren't dead. One of the National Guardsmen that I'd seen had been missing too much of his throat to have survived, and none of the people that they'd shot should have been able to get back up. Ergo, this was no disease. It worked like one at first, yes, but after a certain point, it stopped working like any disease or virus and started working like something else entirely. My brain rejected the word that came to mind next, but as Porsche drove down the darkened road ahead of us, I forced myself to accept it.

Zombies. The Asura virus or whatever it was turned people into cannibalistic zombies. I was right in the middle of the fucking zombie apocalypse.

Chapter 5

Oaths and Anticipation

It is easy to make promises - it is hard work to keep them.

~ Boris Johnson ~

We rounded another curve in the road and Porsche slowed down. Ahead of us was the burning wreck of a sports car that had hit a minivan in the middle of the intersection of Battlefield and Jefferson. Battlefield was a four lane road that ran past the only mall in Springfield, so I'd expected some traffic there, but the wreck complicated everything by closing off the lanes heading east. A few cars were backed up on Jefferson, and I could only guess at how far back Battlefield was jammed up. I crouched back down.

"Take a right into the Kum'N'Go parking lot," I said. "There's a service road that goes further back. Stay on it until you pass the thrift store." She nodded and took the right. The convenience store was dark and empty as we passed it, and I glanced at the fuel gauge on her dash as we passed the gas pumps. She had just over a quarter of a tank, hopefully enough to get us to where we needed to go, and maybe a bit more. Now all we had to do was find a way to get there.

As she made her way through the parking lot, I dropped down to sit in the bed of the truck and pulled my flashlight out of my backpack to take a look at the rifle I'd picked up. It looked like it had seen some wear, but nothing rattled or looked like it was going to fall off. When I'd been in the Air Force, we'd learned how to shoot the M-16A2. I'd even managed to qualify for the Marksmanship ribbon when I shipped to Iraq. It had been a few years since I'd handled one, but I remembered the basics well enough to drop the magazine and reload a new one. I pulled the charging handle to make sure it wasn't jammed, then flipped it over to look at the fire selector. Like the M16A2, this one had three positions: "Safe", "Semi" and "Burst". I set it for semi to conserve ammunition, then ran the light over the rest of the gun. With the telescoping stock and flat receiver top, it looked like I'd grabbed an M4 carbine. It had a short scope mounted on it, and when I looked through it, I could see the illuminated reticle. With that, I'd be able to make most of the thirty rounds in the fresh magazine count, assuming I could hold the rifle steady enough.

Screams came from the apartment complex to my right, accompanied by heavy pounding and the occasional breaking of glass. Movement in the distance behind us caught my eye, but whoever it was never emerged into the light. As Porsche made the turn into the parking lot of the Goodwill Thrift store, I caught a brief glimpse of someone running through the apartment complex as they passed between two buildings. Seconds later, a group of figures sprinted across the same narrow opening. My gut clenched when I heard the screams start a few seconds after that.

I forced myself to turn my attention back to the road as we emerged from between the thrift store and an upscale restaurant. On the far side of the road from us, a line of cars was backed up all the way to the next stop light and beyond. Porsche uttered some choice curse words as I knelt down to look in the rear window.

"We're stuck here," she hissed as she pulled through the parking lot and turned the truck's dented nose into the parking lot's sloped exit. I watched as more and more cars joined the line, then looked back over my shoulder toward the apartment complex.

"Wait for it," I said softly.

"Wait for what?" she asked. To her credit, I saw her flex her hands on the steering wheel.

"Chaos," I said slowly. "Somewhere along this line, some intellectual giant is going to figure out that things will go faster if..." I paused, and my faith in humanity was vindicated by the strident blaring of a car horn. More horns joined in the chorus, and I closed my eyes as a chorus of shrieks rose from behind us.

"Oh, no," Porsche said quietly.

"Someone's going to bolt, and that'll give us a gap," I said as I grabbed the M4 and looked left and right. Figures emerged from the shopping center to our right and charged the waiting cars. More screams erupted down the street as we watched the infected drag people out of their cars and fall on them in the road. I heard gunshots from my right, then the sound I'd been hoping for ripped the night open to my left: the sound of a revving engine and breaking glass. Two car-lengths to our left, a bright yellow Hummer H2 in the right hand lane was shoving a Hyundai Sonata out its way. The smaller car was no match for the massive SUV, and it slid into the middle of the road with a grinding of metal as the Hummer did a U turn and headed back west.

"Go! GO!" I yelled even as Porsche burned rubber out of the parking lot. The truck bounced onto the road, then I was flung against the right side of the bed as she slewed to the left. My back and left shoulder took the impact as my legs flew into the air. Desperately, I grabbed the window frame with my right hand and pulled myself up so I could see where we were going. My first thought was that ignorance had been bliss as we bounced over the curb. Ahead of us was the side of a house.

"Right!" I yelled frantically. "Go right!" Porsche yanked the wheel to the right, and her truck chewed up someone's back lawn as we skidded through something that got us pointed at the gap in the chain-link fence surrounding a playground. Calling it a turn would have been generous. She hit the gas again and we sent a gout of dirt up behind us for a second, then I was pointing to her left.

"There! Behind the school. Cut across the field there. Then go right. That'll bring you out on Kimbrough," I explained. Without waiting for an acknowledgement, I turned and looked over my shoulder. Sure enough, we were being chased. I couldn't tell how many, but the shrieks that were reaching my ears told me that it was too goddamn many. We opened up the distance between our pursuers and our tender behinds as Porsche crossed the playground, but they gained some of it back when she slowed down to make the turn to our right. Chain-link fence blurred by on either side as she poured on speed, and then we were fishtailing our way onto Kimbrough. The shrieks of the infected followed us as she wrestled with the wheel to stay on the road. An intersection loomed ahead, and the headlights illuminated the profile of a man in slacks and a suit jacket in the middle of the road. I felt the truck slow as Porsche took her foot off the gas pedal. In the split second before she could hit the brake, the man turned his head toward us. Blood covered the lower half of his jaw, and thick strands of gore dripped from his chin. A sound of disgust came from Porsche, then the truck surged forward as she hit the gas again and I found myself sliding along the bed of the truck on my side. Pain blossomed in my right shoulder as I hit the tailgate, and a microsecond later, I was bouncing off the floor of the truck as the bed bucked underneath me. My left hand grabbed the tailgate and I pulled myself up in time to see the mangled body of the infected man rolling along for a few seconds in the glow of the tail lights before the darkness swallowed him up again.

My shoulder and back hurt like Hell as I grabbed the M4 and crouch-walked back to the rear window. More shrieks came from either side to our rear as we flew through another intersection.

"Where in the Hell are we going, anyway?" she yelled over her shoulder to me.

:Sunset and Fort," I called back. "Willow Gardens."

"Campbell's gonna be a bitch," she said.

"Probably," I said. "Get on the north side of Sunset. We'll cross the ditch at Jefferson and get on the Greenways trail to avoid traffic."

"You are completely insane, did you know that?"

"It's one of my more endearing traits," I said as I stood up again. This time, I made sure I had a good grip on the lip of the window. Street lights cast an orange glow on the street in front of us, and I could see headlights and tail lights in front of us. It looked like they were all pointed west, but it wasn't until I saw the blur of lights going the opposite way across the intersection that I was sure. We sped through the last stop sign and came up on Sunset. Like Battlefield, Sunset was backed up headed west. Going east, it was pretty much clear. Aside from the one car that we'd seen, no one seemed too interested in going back *into* town. I didn't blame them. Porsche stopped for a second, then turned right onto Sunset.

"What are you doing?" I ducked down to ask.

"Getting on the other side of Sunset," she said with a smile. "Trust me, I've got plan B covered." She headed down Sunset, and beyond the last of the cars, then took a left turn onto a short maintenance road. Once we were past the curb, she turned back to the left, and followed the sidewalk toward a thicket of trees that came to the edge of the concrete. While we bumped along over the grass, I grabbed one of the pistol belts and pulled the Beretta from its holster. The magazine that dropped into my hand had a reassuring weight to it, but I changed it out anyway and chambered a round just in case, then thumbed the hammer down.

"There's a round in the chamber," I said to her as I passed the belt into the cab. "Fifteen rounds of nine millimeter bang-bang in that. Just aim for the head and pull the trigger."

"What about you?" she asked.

"Already got one," I said in an outrageously bad Monty Python accent. "It's verra nice." As I was making hash of British humor, I buckled the other belt around my waist. Her laugh was quick, and I could hear the first hints of hysteria in it. We passed the trees, and Porsche cut across the field that opened up to our right toward Jefferson Street. Luck must have been with us, or maybe we'd managed to fly under its radar, because there weren't a lot of cars on Jefferson. We crossed the bridge that ran over the creek, and she followed the concrete trail as it led behind the trees and sheltered us from sight. Behind us, the shrieking of the infected sounded, and we heard chaos erupt again. I could hear Porsche's voice rising and falling in a steady chant through the window.

"Hold it together, just hold it together, You can do this. Just hold it together," she was muttering to herself. She jumped when I put my hand on her shoulder.

"Porsche. Turn your headlights off. Drive slowly. Inhale, exhale, repeat as necessary…just breathe. We're going to make it."

"What about them?" she asked as she pointed toward the screaming.

"They're in Someone Else's hands now. Our job is to stay alive. I don't know about you, but I have people who are counting on me to be there for them. I don't mean to let them down by getting myself killed."

"I don't have anyone here," she said as she turned her head back to face the trail. "No one to look out for and no one to look out for me. I don't suppose there's room on your list for one more is there?"

"There's always room for one more friend on the list," I said, trying to keep my tone light. "I think you've more than earned it tonight."

"Thanks," she said as the truck slowed to a stop. Campbell loomed ahead of us, with cars backed up as far as we could see from the trail. I stood up so I could get a better view, and found myself at about eye level with the curb because of the Greenways trail's lower elevation. Cars filled all four lanes and every single one of them was pointed south. None of them were moving, though most looked like they were running. Behind us, the shrieks and screams were getting louder as the infected found more victims. I had minutes left to come up with a way past this. My brain raced to find an answer, and when it came to me, it was another cat that delivered it.

As the infected devoured the living, I watched a calico cat emerge from the brush beside us and trot confidently down the trail and follow it under the bridge. Moments later, three half grown kittens scampered after her. The trailway was too narrow, but the spillway beside it was just wide enough for Porsche's truck. It had been right there in front of me the whole time. I squatted down.

"Under the bridge. And don't spare the paintjob." She nodded and put the truck into gear. We hit the concrete spillway and she aimed the nose for the opening in the middle. The thick cement partitions were just barely wide enough to slip between. Her side mirrors scraped against the sides for a few feet before they bent back on themselves. The headlights came on, and she drove us through the darkened passage and out the other side. I let out the breath I'd been holding once the night sky was in view again, and Porsche headed for the right bank of the creek again. She turned her headlights off before she got us back on the Greenways path, and we were on our way again.

The trail led us back to Sunset, and we followed it to where the street became a divided road. There were very few cars on this side of Sunset, and we had no trouble getting into the west bound lanes. It was quiet here, the screams of the dying just a faint whisper in my ear, and all the more sinister for that. I stood back up and leaned against the cab, eyes forward. My girl was less than a mile away, and getting closer every second. The blinking red lights of the intersection were my beacon, and Maya was just beyond them. I could feel my heartbeat faster in my chest as we got closer to the intersection, and my breath seemed to be just a little short.

"When we get to Fort, go right and then take the first street on your left," I directed Porsche through the window. She took the right turn smoothly and eased her way through the left turn. The red brick front of Willow Gardens was barely visible in the lights of the parking lot, but I could see enough to start grinning. We were almost there, and Maya was as good as in my arms again.

And then, the building blew up.

Chapter 6

The Ashes of Faith

Despair is the conclusion of fools.

~ Benjamin Disraeli ~

There is a sound that an explosion makes that is nothing like what you hear on TV or in the movies. Explosions don't have this long, almost crackly sound that goes on forever. It was more of a *whump* that I felt in my chest like a kick from a giant. The truck rolled to a stop as the heat washed over me, and I watched a ball of fire roll into the sky. Porsche's door opened below me. When she got out of the truck, her head turned up to the orange column of smoke and fire that climbed into the night. One hand went to her mouth, then she turned back to me.

"Oh, God," she said. "Dave, I'm so sorry." Something in me tried to die as I watched the building burn, but another part refused to let it. Rage and pain fought each other to get out, but one thing beat them both down: denial. My brain refused to believe Maya was dead. Pure defiance drove me to grab the M-4 and jump out of the bed of the truck. Porsche stepped in front of me and put her hand on my chest.

"Dave, don't do this to yourself," she said softly. "She couldn't have survived that. Nothing could have."

"Denial is the first stage of grief. You don't want to get in the way of that. Not now. Not with me."

"Why not?"

"Because the next stage is anger. Now either come with me or stay here, but whatever you do right now…don't stand in my way." She stepped aside to let me pass. The sound of her truck starting came from behind me as I walked up the driveway into the parking lot. Employee parking was on the right side of the building, and I followed the concrete to where I knew Maya normally parked her car. Broken glass and smoldering bits of debris crunched under my feet as I prowled the side of the building. Most of the cars were on fire, their interiors belching out black smoke and orange flames. The paint was scorched black on all of them, so I was forced to look at the body styles. Minivan, SUV, sedan, another minivan, a compact, all blazing away in the darkness. Behind them, the building burned too, consuming anything that wasn't brick. Movement from inside the building caught my eye, and I saw the silhouette of something vaguely human shaped moving through the flames. It moved toward the windows, then fell into the fire around it. I shuddered as I watched another one walk toward a hole in the wall, then fall into the flames. Something had survived the explosion.

As I realized I was near the end of the row, I started to feel a bit of dread. As much as I wanted to believe she'd somehow survived, or had the foresight to leave before the place blew up, I knew that was hoping for a lot. She'd come in late for a shift, so her car was probably parked near the end of the row. My stomach started to sink as I went. Porsche's truck crawled along behind me, illuminating the ground in front of me. When I came to the empty space, hope made my heart skip a beat. Without thinking, I stepped into the empty spot and stared at the ground, as if I could somehow see Maya's car being parked there. I checked the last two spaces beyond it, and didn't recognize either car as hers. Her car wasn't here. My hope was that she hadn't been here when the building blew, either.

My leg tingled for a moment before I realized my phone was vibrating in my pocket. I slung the M-4 and dug for it. My fingers trembled as I pulled it out and looked at the front screen. *Amy,* it read. Seeing Maya's daughter's name made my heart crumble as I put the phone to my ear. What was I going to tell her?

"Dave, do you know where Mom is? She's not answering her phone!" I heard her say frantically before I could even say hello.

"Amy, what's wrong?" I asked. Telling her that her mother was most likely dead could wait a few minutes, and all I had left was the stupidly obvious.

"Dad's freaking out. He picked me up from school early, and when we got home, he turned out all the lights and grabbed one of his guns and he keeps looking out the window. Dave, I'm scared."

"There's something going on, Amy. Are there strange people walking around in your neighborhood?" I asked.

"I don't know, he won't let me get near the windows. He just told me to go to my room and stay there. What's going on Dave?" For all that she sounded scared, she didn't sound like she'd completely lost it. She was a lot like her mother that way.

"It's some kind of outbreak," I told her after a few seconds' thought. "It's a disease that makes people into cannibals. I'll be there in a few minutes. Grab your go bag and whatever else you can carry. We're getting out of town."

"I don't think Dad'll like that. He's all 'I pay my taxes, where the hell are the police?' and stuff." Her impression of her father was funny enough to get a chuckle out of me.

"Well, what do you want to do?" I asked. There was a pregnant pause on the other end of the line before Amy spoke again.

"I want us to get out of town." Her voice was thick with emotion. I felt bad for asking her to make that decision, but it was her life, too.

"Then get out there and tell him that. And tell him to aim for the head if any of the infected come at you."

"Infected?" she asked.

"You'll know them when you see them. Now go. I'll be there as soon as I can!" I closed the phone.

"What is it?" Porsche asked from her truck.

"That was Maya's daughter Amy. I think there are infected in her neighborhood. We need to go get her."

"What about your girlfriend?" Portia said.

"Her car isn't here. I don't know where she is. If I had to guess, I'd bet she would be trying to get to Amy." I started to go to the truck when something grabbed my right foot. I stumbled and managed to catch myself on my left foot, then I felt something clamp on to the back of my right ankle. Pain spiked up my leg as I looked back to see the red and black upper half of an infected gnawing on my foot. Tattered bits of charred fabric clung to its body, and I could see the band of half melted metal around its left wrist that I figured was a wristwatch once upon a time. I clawed the pistol out of its holster and drew a bead on the top of its head. The gun bucked in my hand, and bits of bone and half-cooked brain matter splattered across the concrete. The muzzle blast was like a slap against my leg, but the pain in my ankle let up.

"Dave!" Porsche yelled as she jumped out of the truck. She was at my side in a heartbeat. I reached down and pulled at my pant leg. It slid up to reveal a thick half-circle of purple on the outside of my Achilles tendon. I twisted my foot to see its mirror image on the inside. I twisted my foot to look at the other side again, then back.

"You've been bitten!" she cried as I looked closer. There were no teeth marks, and no blood. I looked at the infected corpse's mouth and saw no white behind the charred lips.

"Actually," I said with a relieved chuckle, "I've been gummed. Saved by modern dentistry." My leg hurt like hell, but the bite hadn't broken the skin. Still, I wasn't about to take any chances. I pulled out my pocket knife and cut the bottom of my pant leg away to get rid of any saliva. Once I'd cut the cloth free, I got to my feet and limped toward Porsche's truck.

"So, you're not infected?" she asked from beside me. I shook my head and climbed back into the bed of the truck.

"Didn't break the skin. So unless it transmits just from contact, I'm okay. Let's get out of here. The next one that crawls out of that place might not be so dentally deficient." She hopped into the cab pretty quickly at that.

"You sure you don't want to ride up here?" she asked through the back window. "It might be easier on you."

"I'm sure. I like having the wind on my face. I'm like a dog that way." I pulled the nearly spent pistol magazine from my left cargo pocket and thumbed the last round out of it before I stuck the mag back. The other reason I preferred the back of the truck to riding in the cab was the better vantage point. I could look around in a full circle, and I had an unobstructed field of fire.

"Okay, it's your ass. Where to next?" she asked as she started the engine.

"Brentwood Street. It's just the other side of Glenstone," I said while I pulled the M9 out of its holster. The mag dropped into my hand, and I pressed the round I'd stripped from the other magazine into this one to bring the magazine's count back up to fifteen, with number sixteen in the chamber.

"That goes right past Battlefield Mall. That's kind of the opposite of avoiding crowds isn't it?" Porsche asked as she backed up.

"Yeah, we're going to have to thread the needle there. St John's is a little ways north of there, too. Of course, the cemetery is just on the other side of the road, so that's convenient."

"Let's hope we don't need that." She pulled out onto the road and wove her way back toward Sunset, heading the wrong way down the split causeway. Shapes began to emerge from the darkness as the fire drew infected to it like moths. We stayed on the road until it rejoined itself, then followed our own treadmarks back into the grass. When we reached the spillway under Campbell, Porsche barely slowed down. A couple of infected jumped over the railing at us, but hit the cement with grisly crunching sounds as the driver's side mirror snapped off in a shower of sparks. When we burst out the other side, we left a few infected picking themselves up from a cement faceplant on the other side as well. Only one got to its feet. The other three limped along on legs that bent in a couple of extra places. The mostly whole one could *run* though. Porsche got us back on the Greenways trail, and Flash the Infected Sprinter came up with us. I could hear the slap of his feet against the concrete over the hum of the truck, and a rhythmic grunting. We were pulling away, but not fast enough. The minute we slowed down, he'd be on us. I needed to slow him down or kill him.

I brought the M-4 up and tried to sight in on him with the scope. Between the bouncing of the truck and the way his head bobbed around, there was no way I was going to get a clean kill without wasting a ton of ammo. Orange light from the streetlamps filtered through the trees, and I could make out that Flash was wearing a white lab coat over a suit coat, slacks and loafers. In the dark, it was hard to tell much more than that. The truck angled left, and I lost sight of him for a moment. I risked a moment I didn't really have to look over my shoulder at the path in front of us. We had under two hundred feet of straight-away left, and I was guessing only half that in lead time on Flash. When I looked back, he had rounded the curve and was headed our way. *Why are some of them so goddamn fast?* I wondered. Most of the ones we'd seen were slow, like you'd expect from the walking dead. It was why they were called the "walking dead" after all, right? But a few were crazy fast. Like the ones from the hospitals. A half formed theory started to spin in my head.

"Slow down!" I yelled over my shoulder as I flipped the M-4 to burst mode. The truck's engine dropped a pitch, and Flash started getting a lot closer a lot faster. Suddenly calm, I brought the rifle up to my cheek again and tried to place the red dot on Flash's chest. When he was close enough that I was pretty sure I'd hit, I pulled the trigger. The rifle bucked against my shoulder and muzzle flare blotted out everything in front of the scope for less than a second. When I brought the barrel back down, Flash was tumbling along the trail about a hundred feet behind us. He slid to a stop, and I reached back with my right hand to slap against the glass. Mentally I counted off three rounds.

"Stop!" I called. The truck slowed and stopped. Behind the infected doctor I'd just dropped, I could see the rest of the ones who'd jumped after us limping along slowly. There was no way they were going to catch up to us, but I couldn't just leave them up and walking around. I thumbed the fire selector to single shot and took aim at a man in bright red workout gear. My first shot blew the left half of his head away, and I went to the woman in a miniskirt and a tight blue top behind him. *Four,* I counted as I stroked the trigger. She lurched at the last second, and I missed

54

cleanly, then adjusted and fired again. She dropped on the second shot, and I went to the next one. *Five, six, seven,* I added to the count as I put a bullet into the head of a kid with his hat skewed sideways. It took three shots to hit a guy in jeans and a black concert t-shirt, bringing my shot count to ten. Recalling Nate's coaching on one of my weekend trips up to Wyoming, I took a long, slow breath, then brought my sites down on one of the last two. He lurched along, and after a couple of steps, I could predict his rhythm. The gun bucked against my shoulder, and he went down. *Eleven.* The last one rounded the corner, a woman in nurse's scrubs. My breath caught as I saw a flash of black hair like Maya's. Was it her? *Too skinny, too tall, no tattoo on her arm.* My finger stroked the trigger, and she went down. *Twelve.*

Finally, Flash started to move. His head came up and he slowly pushed himself to his feet. The front of his white lab coat was stained dark with his own blood, but when he started moving, it was with the slow, lurching movements of the six infected I'd just killed. I put round number thirteen through his forehead and turned to Porsche.

"Alright, let's go," I said with a sense of satisfaction. She gunned the engine and the truck surged forward. We sped across the road and back onto the grass again. From both sides of us, I could hear screams and the occasional gunshot from a distance. The road to our right was eerily quiet, though. I kept my eyes on the line of cars as we sped along the concrete trail. The line was more random now, and there were gaps in it that hadn't been there before. A few cars showed body damage, and more than a couple of them were burning. As we passed a dark colored Volkswagen, I could see someone inside, flailing at the glass. There was a pop and the almost musical tinkling of glass as the driver's side window shattered, then the sound of an enraged, inhuman scream ripped through the night. Even as I felt a shudder run between my shoulder blades, I put the new knowledge into a spot in my head, and gave it a name. The fast, feral infected were ghouls. The slow ones were zombies. The most frightening thing was that the ghouls still seemed to be alive.

We were close to the line of trees that marked the drainage ditch we'd skirted when I heard a deep bass sound, like the rapid thumping of a helicopter, but not like the St. John's Life Flite. This was faster sounding, and louder. A black shape loomed over the houses across Sunset and flew north, blotting out a part of the night sky for a few seconds as it went overhead. Twin rotors at the front and back held the long body aloft, and I heard the familiar whine of a turbine engine. A Chinook, flying with no running lights and no markings that I could see. I filed it away as one more entry on a list of weird shit that was getting longer and longer by the second. We cleared the edge of the trees and for some reason, I felt a little safer as soon as we were out of the black chopper's line of sight. Porsche wasted no time getting back on the trail, and soon we were heading toward the cover of trees.

We slipped past the first branches and found ourselves looking at more asphalt. The Greenways trail paralleled a residential street here, and for almost a quarter of a mile, it looked like we would be exposed on the left. I leaned forward and stuck my face near the opening in the cab's rear window.

"Turn your headlights off and stay on the trailway," I said softly. "Go slowly." Porsche nodded and switched the lights off. The trees grew thick enough overhead that the trail was mostly in shadow, but the streetlights gave us enough illumination to see where we were going. I stayed hunkered down by the back window as we coasted along. Off to our left, a row of apartments loomed, the windows darkened and eerily silent. We crept past quietly, and an agonizingly slow two or three minutes later the trail led back into the trees. Sunset angled closer on our right, and I could see more movement on the road through the trees. Porsche kept the headlights off as she sped up a little, trusting to the narrow bands of light that bled through the leaves to show us where the trail was. Ahead, we could hear the screeching of tires; it ended with the unmistakable *crump* of cars hitting each other at speed.

When the trees began to thin out, we could see a knot of cars stopped on National and the sound of raised voices. The road itself looked clear on either side of them, and as we got closer, it looked like your average pileup. A light colored little hybrid was on its side in the middle of the road, with the rear end of a Caddy sticking out from behind the front of it. I could see the back end of a truck jutting out from behind the rear end and another car with its nose buried under the truck's rear bumper.

Gunshots shattered the argument, and I saw a body fall to the pavement on the far side of the truck as I looked under it. A skinny guy with a jumble of tattoos on his lanky arms in a loose wife beater shirt and ripped jeans that threatened to fall off his hips walked around the back of the Caddy while someone else walked behind the truck. The tattooed gangster wannabe peered in the windshield of the hybrid, then stepped back and pulled a chromed revolver into view. The gun boomed four times as he pumped his arm into each shot. Five more pops from another gun corresponded to five flashes of light from the other side of the car jammed under the truck's bumper.

"You're dead, bitch!" the skinny guy crowed as he gestured with the gun. The other guy came around from behind the far end of the pile up with an automatic held high and sideways in his right hand. He was wearing loose pants of his own that drooped around his hips, and a button down shirt over a white wife beater, with a baseball hat worn with the flat bill off to one side.

"Killed that motherfucker!" he yelled to his friend. The two examples of Rule Twelve met near the middle of the vehicles and started talking. From fifty yards away, I couldn't make out what they were saying, but they gestured at the cars. I was guessing their wannabe pimp-mobile was totaled. Judging by the headshaking that was going on, I was willing to bet that the other three cars were out of commission, too. Porsche and I stayed still as they started looking around. The skinny guy with the revolver pointed to the north, and I glanced that way. Movement caught my eye, and I uttered a whispered curse.

"Dumbasses," Porsche hissed from in the cab. I agreed silently and hoped they were going to take off running. But then the kid in the button down shirt turned toward us. He started walking our way and raised the pistol homey-style, gun sideways, held up almost over his head.

"Bitch, you better get out my truck!" he yelled as he strode toward us sounding like a walking stereotype. It was time to introduce this would be bad-ass to Dave's Rule Number Fourteen: Guns are not magic wands. Pointing one at someone didn't mean they were automatically going to do what you told them to.

"Get down," I whispered, "and light him up." She leaned across the seat and reached for the light controls on the steering column. The headlights caught Hat Wannabe flatfooted and he squinted against the sudden light. Then he started popping off rounds our way.

"You did NOT just flash that shit in my face, bitch!" he said as he fired. Bullets whizzed by us, but only one actually hit the truck, proving that readiness to pull the trigger did not equal any ability to actually hit what you were shooting at. The gun stopped making noise, and I surged to my feet. Unlike the two thugs, I was not too cool to use the sights, and I knew how to hit what I shot at. They were about to learn a hard lesson in cause and effect: shooting at someone means that they just might shoot back. Hat Wannabe was framed in the cone of light as he tried to drop the magazine from his pistol. Behind him, I could see his buddy bringing his hand cannon up. Time slowed for me as I brought the M4 up and tried to put the red dot in the optic in the middle of his chest. When I got it dancing around more or less where I wanted it, I pulled the trigger twice. He dropped like a rag doll, and I moved the sight to Six Gun. *Fourteen, fifteen.* His gun boomed and I heard a bullet whine by as it ricocheted off something. I pulled the trigger again, but he stayed up, so I tried again, and this time sent him spinning. *Sixteen, seventeen.*

"You okay?" I called out to Porsche, my heart hammering in my chest.

"Yeah, I'm fine!" Porsche said, relief plain in her voice as she got herself upright again.

"Get us out of here!" I said as I dropped back down. She wasted no time in putting the truck into gear and leaving fresh ruts in the grass. We bounced off the curb and onto National, then she was making a hard right as we went around the nose of the hybrid. Six Gun was trying to crawl toward his shiny pistol, and Porsche swerved in his direction. He gave out a strangled scream as the front wheel hit him, then went silent when the back wheel got him.

"Asshole," I heard Porsche call out as she powered the truck into a sharper left than I thought possible under the laws of physics as I understood them. Once I was done bouncing off the side of the truck bed, I pulled myself up to see that we were barreling down Sunset. The street was empty, so even though we were going the wrong way down the divided road, there wasn't much chance of us hitting someone else coming the other way. We crossed over to the right side of the road as soon as it merged back to four lanes again, and slowed down enough to make sure we wouldn't get sideswiped when we crossed Fremont, the next big road. Porsche turned her headlights off as we blazed through the intersection, and we coasted forward quietly.

More screams came from our left, but to our right, it was silent. Trees lined the street on that side for about two hundred yards, cutting off my view of the park. I knew from countless past trips that an empty swimming pool took up this corner of the park. A little further down the road was a playground and a parking lot. I hoped that there was no one out tonight. The thought of zombie kids in softball uniforms sickened me. It took me a moment to realize that it wasn't just the thought of dead kids lurching around. It was the thought that followed: I'd shoot them to stay alive. It bothered me that my brain was even able to envision doing that. Still, I kept sweeping left and right for movement.

Porsche slowed to a stop as we got past the edge of the trees, and I focused forward. Nothing was directly in front of us, but up ahead at the Glenstone intersection, I could see what made her stop. Truth was I should have expected this. Glenstone was one of the major roads through town. It made sense that it would be one of the most backed up roads right now. I could see three cars on fire, and the glow from more fires flickered through the windows and off the paint of other cars further to the south. Silhouetted against the glow were several figures that seemed to be wandering back and forth among the vehicles.

"Well, we're not going that way," Porsche said with an upbeat tone.

"Damn straight. Fremont looked pretty clear, and I think we can get past the hospital by taking one of the side streets."

"We can," she said as she shifted the truck into reverse. The back tire bumped over the almost nonexistent curb before she stopped and shifted back into gear. "I used to live in the apartments at the corner of Fremont and Seminole." She took us back toward Fremont and turned right. According to the mental map I had of this area, she would have lived caddy-corner to the southeast corner of the hospital campus. I hoped she knew what she was doing, because I'd only been through this area a few times, and I didn't trust my memory of it in the dark.

As we pulled even with the first street on the right, screams pierced the night, and we could see shapes emerging onto the road. Porsche straightened the wheel and hit the gas. The next road looked deserted, and she took the turn. As we started down the street, movement on either side caught my attention, but we were going too fast for me to make out what it was. I had a sneaking suspicion, though. Frantic barking broke out ahead of us, and I felt the truck slow. As we got closer, I could see something moving up ahead of us, and the barking got louder. Then I heard something in the dog's barking that made my gut clench up. In between barks, it would let out a whine, then bark again. We pulled up until the dog was to our right, and I dug my flashlight out of my backpack. The cone of light showed a Rottweiler in front of one of the infected. The infected was sitting up slowly, and the dog was down with its forelegs in front of it but it's haunches up in the air. I caught sight of its tail, and gave a smile of approval for its former owner. Most people bobbed the tails on Rott's, but this big fella had his intact. I felt a surge of pity for the poor creature. The Rottweiler was a very devoted breed, and if I was any judge, this one was trying to make sense of what its human had become. It looked at me, then back at the thing that was struggling to its feet in front of it.

There is a saying from the Hagakure, The Book of the Samurai, that one should make decisions within the space of seven breaths. It took me less than one to jump over the side of the truck. I went around to the back and pulled the tailgate down. The dog backed away from the infected, and I let out a whistle.

"Come on, boy!" I called out. It gave a low whine, then ran toward a pile of things in front of the house behind it. My jaw dropped in disbelief as it carried a rolled up green wool blanket back in its mouth. Barely breaking stride, it jumped into the back of the truck, then turned around and dropped the blanket at its feet. I closed the tailgate and hopped back in, fighting the urge to go back and bash his former owner's skull in.

"Picking up more strays?" Porsche asked as she gunned the accelerator. I could hear the smile in her voice. The dog gave my proffered hand an experimental sniff before laying eight feet of slobbery tongue across it in what I guessed was his canine approval. I chuckled as I patted his shoulder. A thick leather collar encircled his neck, and I followed it around until I found the tag.

"Sherman," I read aloud. He gave me a short bark in reply. The name fit. Up close, I could see how broad he was across the shoulders. Like the tank he was named for. He laid his head down on his paws and looked up at me with big, soulful doggy eyes, and I imagined I could see the sadness behind them. I ran my hand along his back as I looked out the front windshield at the perilous new world that was being born around us.

Even humans who hadn't been infected were preying on their own kind. As much as I wanted to judge myself superior to the two men I'd shot earlier, in truth, I couldn't say I was that much different. It had been way too easy to pull the trigger the first time, and even easier the second. My gaze went to Sherman as he nuzzled my hand. If there was one difference, though, he was the result of it. My father had always said that you could tell a lot about the character of a man by the way he treated folks around him when he held power in his hands. When we'd had the chance, Porsche and I had helped Sherman out. It was a small difference, but it was enough for me to hang on to my humanity.

Chapter 7

Average, Ordinary Heroes

Unhappy the land in need of heroes

~ *Bertolt Brecht* ~

We drove along quietly after that, Sherman leaning up against me as I rode in the back of the truck, Porsche quiet in the front. All told it had been only a couple of hours since the world started its one way trip to Hell, but already I was feeling the strain. She wound her way through the back streets, and I could hear the moans of the infected and the distant screams of the dying. Gunshots sounded in the distance, and I heard another Chinook fly overhead. That sound stirred questions in my head. What in the Hell were Army helicopters doing flying over the city without their running lights on?

"Turn the radio on," I said. A heartbeat later, static filled the air. Porsche turned the volume down before she turned to me.

"The Q's off the air," she said.

"Try KTTZ," I told her. "If it's news you know they're gonna be all over it." She hit one of the presets on her radio, and an unfamiliar voice came over the speakers.

"...again, evacuation is in progress. Army National Guard personnel and Homeland Security agents are asking all citizens for their cooperation as they evacuate uninfected members of the population. If you have encountered an infected person, please inform the soldiers or agents who are evacuating you and medical help will be provided for you. If you are in a safe place, such as a school or your place of employment, please stay where you are and call this station or 417-555-EVAC. Emergency evacuation is in progress. Stay indoors and do not make contact with anyone who is infected." Silence followed, then the voice began again. "Citizens of Springfield, please stay in your homes and cooperate fully with your local, state and federal government representatives. Martial law has been declared for the state of Missouri and an immediate curfew is in effect. Looters will be shot on sight. Emergency evacuation is in progress. Again, emergency evacuation is in progress. Army National Guard personnel-" Porsche turned the radio off as it started to repeat what we'd already heard, then turned to me with wide eyes full of questions.

"Should we...?" she let the question hang in the air between us. I shook my head slowly.

"No, if this was legit...we'd be seeing running lights on those choppers overhead," I said. "This doesn't feel right." She nodded, and I felt a pang of guilt when she turned her attention back to the road. Up until today, we'd just been co-workers, sharing a few hours at a time, talking about inconsequential things. Now, she was trusting me with her life.

We made a left, then she took a right down a side street and a hundred yards later, we were turning right on to Seminole. The street was clear ahead, save for a few bodies. When we passed the first one, a man in what was left of a patient's hospital gown, I saw tire marks across the side of its head in the pale light of the street lamp. Further on, one of the infected in a white lab coat and suit pants had been reduced to crawling along, its legs and hips twisted almost completely around. Tire marks were clearly visible along its back, and there was broken glass imbedded in its face. A third body was splayed out in the middle of the road, with a bloody tire tread running straight up the back of her skimpy yellow minidress. A grim smile creased my face as I let a spark of hope kindle in my heart. Someone had been this way not long before, and I was willing to put good money on my girl Maya. How she'd gotten past Campbell and the St John's campus was a mystery to me, but if anyone would have been able to figure it out, that person would have been Maya. Glenstone looked like it was still backed up, but I saw an opening a little ways to the left as we got closer. I pointed over Porsche's shoulder, and she nodded. Moments later, she was taking the left turn into the parking lot of a liquor store, then cutting across the lot of an old gas station that had been converted to an auto glass shop. The driveway out of their parking lot led into the narrow opening between two compact cars that were at an angle to the lane they should have been in. Broken glass and shards of black fiberglass littered the edges of the opening, and I could see two strips of black where someone had left a layer of rubber on the concrete. The rear of another car had been pushed out of the way in the next lane, and then the way was clear. I felt a moment of pity for anything between Maya and Amy as I surveyed what I figured was her handiwork. We sped across the empty northbound lanes, into the parking lot of a shopping center I'd passed a million times without ever going in, and cut behind a motorsport shop. I pointed across Seminole to the street that angled between the big community blood bank and the Brentwood Branch of the library. She followed my directions, and in seconds, she had us heading down Brentwood.

"Stay on this street. It'll branch, take the left fork and follow it around to the right after that!" I called to her as she sped along the road.

"Nice neighborhood," she said as we rounded the first curve.

"Yeah, her ex is a lawyer; he specializes in insurance cases."

"That explains a lot," she said with a soft chuckle. She followed my directions to the letter, and in less than two minutes, we were pulling into the driveway of Maya's ex-husband's house. Karl had done well for himself, and his house was in one of the older, upper middle class neighborhoods. It was one of the old Federal style house plans, with tall columns in front and a driveway that went past the left side of the house to a detached three car garage in the back yard. My heart leaped when I saw Maya's battered black car was parked next to the house, and I could hear the faint sound of voices coming from inside as Porsche turned the truck's engine off. Sherman followed me when I jumped over the side of the truck. Porsche was climbing out as well, and I took a moment to assess the area. Rule seven was to know your terrain, and I was making sure I did.

"Okay, I need you to stay alert out here," I told her. "Rule Twelve. Assume that people suck after shit hits the fan, and that they're after your stuff. If you see anyone, let me know."

"I think I figured that one out for myself the hard way back at the park," she said quietly.

"Yeah, you did. Dave's Rule Number Thirteen: Don't be one of the people who suck after shit hits the fan. I'll be back out as soon as I can, and we'll work on getting the hell out of town." She gave me a quick nod, then stepped past me. Sherman followed me to the front door, his claws clicking on the sidewalk. The front door opened when I was a few steps away, and Amy barreled into me with a hug that made my ribs creak. From behind her came raised voices, easily audible until the door shut.

"Thank God you're here!" she murmured into my chest. I put my free arm around her shoulders and pulled her close, then reluctantly let go. Affection was all well and good, and I wanted nothing more than to hug the stuffing out of her, but not when I was carrying an assault rifle. She stepped back and I found myself looking into dark eyes that reminded me of Maya's. Most of her features favored her mother, in fact, from the wavy dark hair to the high cheekbones her distant Cherokee ancestors had gifted her. She might not have been my blood, but when it came down to it, I loved her as if she was my daughter. She and Maya were the reason behind Dave's Rule Number Twenty Two: Watch out for your friends and family. No part of my survival prep had been more important.

"Sounds like they're really going at it," I said as I heard the muffled voices even through the door. "How long ago did your mom get here?"

"Like ten minutes ago." She turned and headed back for the door, leaving me to follow.

"Man, that escalated quickly," I said as I heard Karl's voice from inside.

"Yeah, they pretty much started yelling at each other the second Mom walked in the door. I tried telling Dad what you said, but he wouldn't listen. Once Mom showed up, I didn't even try to get between them." She opened the door, and we were inundated by Karl's booming voice as soon as we walked in the house. I noticed the black backpack sitting next to Maya's purse on the table in the foyer as we headed for the dining room. I felt a sense of pride seeing that she'd had grabbed the bug-out bag from her car. I added 'good partner for the zombie apocalypse' to the list of reasons I'd made a damn good choice in her.

"I don't care what that crackpot loser you're shacked up with says, we're staying *here!* I'm her father and her custodial parent and my word is the only one that counts! You gave up any right to dictate anything about her life when you walked out on us!" He was looming over Maya with his face inches from hers, shouting at the top of his lungs with a gun in his right hand. With anyone else, it might have been intimidating. Against Maya, it was like water on rocks. In a thousand years, it might wear her down a little. Karl was a big man, standing an easy six feet four inches to Maya's five and a half feet. Success had turned him from a muscular man into a beefy one, softening the edges of his features and giving his face a rounder, fuller look to go with the perfectly coiffed hairdo. Maya, on the other hand, was still lean and her face held every well-defined line that I'd fallen in love with when I first met her. Her dark eyes were blazing as she looked up at Karl, and I knew he'd made a mistake.

"I wasn't the one fucking my secretary!" she hissed. "I wasn't the one who left his daughter to shack up with the bitch for six months until he could get custody. I didn't give any of my rights up, you son of a bitch! You stole them from me! And I'm not the idiot who's going to wait for help that's never gonna come!" Something in Karl's face changed, and I saw his hand draw back. My body tensed to move, but Sherman's low growl stopped everyone in the room cold. Karl turned to face me, and his expression transformed into a sneer of disgust.

"Get that dog out of my house before I shoot it," he said as he pointed his pistol at Sherman. I recognized the gun from one of our previous encounters. I'd been on the same side of it then, too. He'd waved the same Colt Python in my face during a drunken tirade the first time I'd brought Amy back home from Thanksgiving three years ago. I hadn't been anywhere near as well armed then as I was now, and it took him a second to realize that he was on the losing end of the pissing contest this time. The pistol wavered for a moment, then slowly lowered as he gave a barely audible gulp.

"Yes, Karl, my dick's bigger today," I said as I stepped into the room, deliberately keeping the barrel of the M-4 pointed down and away from anyone. "Now, we're going to deal with this like reasonable people. The guy with the big gun is going to talk, and you're going to hear him out."

"You're going to jail for this," Karl said. I hefted the M-4.

"Big gun. Talking. Now shut up and listen." I turned to Amy. "Amy, what do you want to do?"

"I want to leave, Daddy," she said in a wavering voice. "I'm scared, and I don't think anyone's going to come help us and I want you to come with us!"

Both Maya and Karl wilted at her words, and Maya rushed to her side. Karl might have been a grade A buttmunch, but where his daughter was concerned, he was still a man trying to be the best father he knew how to be. Even if the best he knew how to be was an asshole, I still had to give him credit for the effort. I slung the carbine and closed the distance between us.

"See, that wasn't so hard. So, what's it going to be?" I asked quietly.

"I refuse to simply flee like lemmings. The roads are blocked, and even if we could get through, we don't stand a chance of making it past the city limits. Even if we could make it *that* far, where do you think we'd go?" He tried staring me down from his greater height, but after the things I'd seen and done in the last two hours, five or six inches of vertical advantage just wasn't enough to get the job done.

"Don't worry, I've got the where covered. And if Maya can make it here from halfway across town, unarmed and alone, why is a big man like you pissing himself over leaving the house?" He puffed up at that, and I knew I'd hit him right where he lived: his pride.

"The government has imposed martial law. I'm not about to let my daughter get herself shot following you," he growled at me.

"Because starvation and disease are much slower deaths for her," I shot back. "And you want her to suffer for as long as possible, right? Look Karl, there is no help coming. None. This is happening nationwide, and we're one of the last cities to be affected. There is almost nothing left to spare by now."

"But…they said on the radio…they're evacuating people," he stammered. I felt as much as heard Amy and Maya come up behind me.

"Dad, come on," Amy said with all the sarcasm inherent in her teenaged body. "They didn't tell anyone what to do or where to go. It's all just 'Stay put and wait.' Where's the evacuation centers?" If there was one expert in the room on being lied to by adults, it was Amy.

"Listen to your daughter, Karl," Maya said gently. "You raised a smart girl…with a little help." He gave us all a glare that melted against the collected wills of the three people staring back at him, then he sort of deflated.

"Alright," he huffed. "Give me a few minutes to get some stuff packed, and we'll go with you." He left the room with a long suffering sigh, and I turned to Amy.

"Way to go there, munchkin," I told her as I gestured for her to come to me. She gave me a quick, tight hug before she backed away to regain her teen composure.

"Thanks," she said.

"Got your go bag ready?" I asked.

"Yeah, it's by my door. I'll be right back." She turned and scampered down the hallway. I held one arm out for Maya, and she wrapped both of hers around me, gun and all. I held her tight and enjoyed the way her form fit against me. I never got tired of the way her body felt pressed up against mine.

"I was so goddamn worried about you," I whispered in her ear. "Why didn't you answer your phone?" Any answer I had hoped for got shoved to the back of the line when she turned her head up and kissed me hard. Or maybe it was me kissing *her* hard. Could've been mutual, too. My lips tingled as we broke the kiss, and I leaned back down to brush my lips against hers for a moment before letting her get completely away.

"You look so damn hot right now," she whispered to me with a mischievous smile. "All rugged and bad-ass."

"No, I don't, and this is so not the time," I whispered back, but my dumbass grin stole all of the seriousness from my voice. "Phone, didn't answer it, still not with the why."

"Oh, that. The cops took it."

"They were at Willow Gardens, too?" I asked.

"Yeah, right up until the first resident died. They showed up about twenty minutes after I got there and searched us, then the bastards went through our lockers. They took cell phones, tablets, everything. If I hadn't stashed my Kindle in the med cart, they would have tried to grab it, too."

"Doesn't surprise me. We had a cop and a sheriff's deputy at Prov-Am."

"I *think* ours were Springfield police. Their uniforms were the right color, but they had those vests on, and they cleared out when the first resident coded. I never did get close enough to get a good look at them." My brain went back to the man in the black uniform I'd seen back at Prov-Am. My guess at the time had been Springfield PD as well, but something wasn't adding up for me. My brain wasn't producing any immediate answers, so I let the question slide back to the back of my mind while I focused on the more here and now problems.

"Well, by this time tomorrow, it's going to be a moot point. We'll be half way to Wyoming by tomorrow night," I said with more confidence than I had any right to have.

"God I hope so. What happened to your leg?" I looked down at the shortened pant leg that had given me away, then back up at her with a weak smile.

"I almost got bit. If they'd had teeth, we wouldn't be having this reunion right now. I cut the pant leg away to get rid of the zombie spit."

"We'd better disinfect your leg, too," she said as she started pulling me toward the hallway.

"Why not use the first aid kit in your bag?" I asked as she pulled me into the bathroom and pointed at the toilet seat. I sat while she raided Karl's medicine cabinet. I'd learned a long time ago to trust Maya, and one place I always followed her lead in was anything medical. She'd been a certified nurse's assistant, a surgical technician and most recently, she'd gone back to working rehab as a certified med-tech. While she wasn't anywhere close to a doctor, she knew her way around the human body a lot better than I did.

"Use what's around you before you start digging in to your own supplies," she said with a smile as she sat on the edge of the tub facing me. She already had a pair of latex gloves on and was looking my ankle over with a critical eye. "You taught me that, baby. Besides, I've been paying that bastard child support for six years, it's about time I got a little back." She ripped open a sterile gauze pad, grabbed a bottle of hydrogen peroxide from the counter beside me and pressed the white square to the opening before she upended the brown bottle. She gently wiped the area around the bruise and then the bruise itself while I winced. Fortunately, I didn't feel the sting of an open wound as a thin white foam built up under the pad, which made me feel better on two levels when she grabbed the bottle of rubbing alcohol. One, I knew for sure that I wasn't infected, and two, it wasn't going to smart when she wiped the area down with the alcohol. The gauze pad felt cool against my skin, and I noticed tiny gray flakes in the foam on the first pad she'd used.

"Will I ever play football again, doc?" I asked.

"It's going to leave one hell of a bruise," she said flatly, then she turned the full force of her most concerned look on me. "You have no idea how lucky you were. Even without teeth, they could have damaged your Achilles tendon. Damn it Dave, be careful!"

71

"It's the freaking zombie apocalypse. One of the few things I *didn't* plan for seriously." I stood up and pulled her to me, for a moment feeling the stress of the past few hours catching up to me. "I'm doing the best I know how, but I can't tell you how far behind the curve I am on this, babe. And I hate it." I gave her a quick kiss and stepped back.

"You're doing great," she told me. "We're still alive, so I guess we're doing better than a lot of other people, right?" I nodded and smiled in spite of myself.

"Okay, let's break up this little pity party and get back to the business of surviving. Go ahead and raid his medicine cabinet, I'll hit his pantry and help him get ready to bug out after I get my ride to come inside."

"Your ride?" she asked.

"Yeah. I didn't walk all this way this fast. One of my coworkers gave me a ride. Her name's Porsche and she saved my ass at least once tonight."

"Porsche? Like the porn star?" she said dubiously.

"I was thinking like the car company, but I guess the spelling's the same. And how do you know *that*?"

"I'm not a nun, honey. You'd never believe some of the stuff that used to come up when I worked overnights. Why did you make her wait outside?"

"Because I didn't want to bring her into a war zone by way of introduction to you and Karl," I answered. That got me a glare that I ignored with a promise to be right back.

Amy was waiting by the door with her bug-out bag and another duffel bag ready. Her go-bag was the same unadorned black backpack as Maya's, with a flashlight and a water bottle in the outside mesh pockets. Her duffle bag was a blue Nike set up with a long shoulder strap. The two shorter handle straps were buttoned together over a much-loved teddy bear. Even at fourteen, there was still just a touch of the little girl who'd first won my heart four years before. I gave her shoulder a squeeze before I opened the door and went out to Porsche's truck.

"All clear so far," she said as I came up beside the truck. "How are things on the domestic front lines?"

"We've declared a ceasefire, but I'm not sure how long it'll hold. Grab your duffle and come on inside. We're going to get you a little better stocked before we head out."

"Dave, you've already done plenty for me," she said, shaking her head. "I'm fine."

"I'm calling bullshit on that, and playing the 'I insist' card. That trumps all protests. Now come on. I need your help inside." She rolled her eyes at me but she followed me in.

Maya had a plastic container on the table that she was busy sorting through, and I could hear someone going through the cabinets in the kitchen. She looked up as I came in, and her eyes fell on Porsche. I watched as they did the mutual scan. Maya's eyes went to clothes first, while Porsche's went to Maya's face. I could imagine what was going through their respective minds. Maya was evaluating Porsche for the skank factor, I figured. The professional clothes that didn't bare half of her tits for public consumption probably earned points in Porsche's favor, while the tight stretch pants were being moderately offset by the low-heeled ankle boots. Porsche, on the other hand, was probably looking for the flare up of the jealous girlfriend syndrome and not understanding why it wasn't happening.

"Porsche, this is my girlfriend Maya. Maya, this is Porsche. Both of you play nice." That earned me a dark look from both of them, and I smiled. At least they agreed on something.

"Hi," Porsche said as she stepped forward. "Dave and I sit across the aisle from each other at work. He talks about you all the time." Maya offered her a disbelieving smile and nodded.

"Pleased to meet you," she said stiffly. Just then, Amy wandered out of the kitchen with a blue plastic tub in her hands. She set it on the table with a clank and started rooting around in the bottom without looking up.

"Mom, do you still have that regular can opener at your place? I think Dad threw ours out." The tense moment evaporated as she looked up in total innocence and noticed

Porsche. "Did I interrupt a grown up thing or something?" she asked.

"No, your mom was just telling Porsche she was pleased to meet the girl who rescued me earlier tonight. When I found myself in the middle of a group of zombies."

"Right, Plan B. When you screamed like a little girl?" Porsche asked.

"Oh, God!" Maya said. "Did he give you that bit about plan A never works?" They laughed as they found a little common ground at my expense. I left them to talk for a few moments and went over to Amy.

"The kitchen's pretty much cleared out," she said. "It's pretty much soup, veggies and Ramen noodles." The plastic tub she'd brought in was half full of cans and plastic packages. The kitchen cabinets were standing open, and were largely bare.

"What about staples? Flour, sugar and salt?" I asked. It didn't make sense that Amy would miss that.

"We had a little bit of sugar and salt, but no flour. If it isn't delivered or come ready to cook in the microwave, Dad doesn't buy it. Most of the time we just eat out anyway." I shook my head.

"It's a wonder you're as healthy as you are. So, do you have any camping gear or outdoorsy stuff?"

"Do we ever," she said. "Mom, Dave and I are going out to the garage," she called out. Maya gave an affirmative, and Amy led me out the back door. The bulk of Karl's back yard was concrete driveway, though the right rear corner had a grassy little rise on it with an old oak growing in the corner. A cute miniature house sat under it, and I remembered Amy calling it her playhouse. The rest of the back side of the yard was dominated by a two level, three car garage. Amy led us in through a side door and flipped on the lights. The sight before me instantly gave me a bad case of auto envy. Karl's green Range Rover sat at the far end, dwarfing the red Jaguar that took up the middle spot. The Jag was completely useless for anything right now, but I still drooled a little as Amy led me up the wooden staircase at the rear of the garage. I took note of the three bicycles that were hanging upside down from the ceiling beside the staircase, and gave one of the wheels a squeeze. It was still firm under pressure. Whatever his other failings, Karl knew how to take care of his stuff.

The upper level was a tribute to Karl's premature mid-life syndrome. He had too many things going on to just call it a crisis, and the cast-offs of his abandoned attempts at recapturing his youth had been exiled to the upper level of the garage. The back wall had been turned into one long work bench that he'd stocked with a complete set of automotive and woodworking tools. The far end was home to four freestanding shelving units that were stacked with boxes, most of them stamped with Bass Pro and Coleman logos.

"Remember when Dad spent those two summers taking me and Sabrina camping?" she said as she crossed the floor. "Turns out, his idea of roughing it included electrical hookups and outdoor showers." I took stock of the boxes, mentally tossing more than half of the stuff. Air mattresses, pumps for the air mattresses, a huge cook stove and chuck-box, cots and some sort of bug repelling device all went into the mental trash. So did the monstrously over-sized McMansion of a tent. A smaller Coleman camp stove and a compact set of cookware caught my eye; I pulled them off the shelf and handed them to Amy. She set them on the workbench and made it back in time to catch the oversized sleeping bag I tossed her way. The camp stools and other amenities were unnecessary weight for what I had in mind, so they were left on the shelves. Besides, sacrificing them made more room for the camping first aid kit, the Dutch oven and its tripod. The rest of the camping gear duplicated things I already had better versions of, so I left them on the shelves as well.

"Okay, not the most productive trip, but nothing lost for it…except a little of your Dad's pride."

"He's got ego to spare," Amy said as we carted our spoils down the steps. "Let me get my camping gear, and I'll be ready to go."

"Ooookay," I said with a thumb pointed over my shoulder "Whose gear did we just go through?"

"That was Dad and Sabrina's crap. Dad let me get my own stuff. Probably saved someone's life."

"Yours or his?" I asked.

"Sabrina's. I couldn't stand that whiny bitch, but don't tell Mom I said that."

"I'm a vault." She nodded and headed toward the little playhouse. Less than a minute later, she came back with a big backpack slung over one shoulder. She grabbed her share of the gear again and started for the back door. We stepped into the dining room to see Karl shaking his head as Maya was giving him one of her rare approving looks over a plastic tub full of first aid supplies.

"No, I don't recognize it. I just bought the big camping first aid kit from Bass Pro," he said. Her approving look faded back to the usual slightly bemused look that was the best she usually got around him. I slid the first aid kit across the table to Maya.

"I made it, Mom," Amy said as we dumped the rest of the gear on the table. Karl winced when the Dutch oven clattered across the cherry wood table's smooth finish.

"Good job," Maya said with a smile. "I thought it looked like something I'd made."

"I read about it on Dave's website, and I thought it would be a good idea. Especially when Dad sliced his finger open on a can lid last Thanksgiving."

"I put his website on the parental control list on my firewall. How did you go to it?" Karl demanded.

"Oh, please, Daddy," Amy said. "I figured out how to get around that months ago."

"We're going to have a serious talk about…Maya, what are you doing?" His face was turning red as he reached for the contents of the camping first aid kit that Maya had dumped on the table. She slapped his hands away and started sorting through the stuff.

"Getting rid of the useless crap," she said as she tossed the first aid booklet and a couple of packets of decongestant pills aside. "Decongestants, antacids, sting relief, those are for comfort, not treating serious injuries. Band-Aids, they're good for covering a cut or a scrape but they're shit for something bigger than that. And sunscreen? Please, Karl, that isn't first aid, that's Bass Pro trying to come up with crap to pad their kit with." He stood back and fumed as she tore the kit apart. I knew if I let him stand around with nothing to do, his mouth was likely to go off.

"Karl, show me what you packed," I said as I came around the table to him.

"Why? So you can tell me what I did wrong?" he sulked.

"No, so I know what you're bringing. The more familiar we are with each other's gear, the better equipped we are to make decisions." I matched his gaze with a calm look, and he set his duffel bag on the table. I nodded approvingly, and he unzipped it. He had the essentials. Underwear, socks, hygiene stuff. A few changes of clothes, nothing formal. In the bottom of the bag, though, were the real treasures. A bottle of scotch, Glenlivet to be exact, a bottle of Jack Daniel's Black Label and a bottle of Crown Royal lay side by side underneath his clothes, padded by socks. A box of .45 caliber rounds was packed neatly beside three boxes of Remington .223 rounds.

"Well?" he said as I shuffled through his stuff.

"Good choices for the booze," I said as I looked up at him. "And I see you went with that Mini-14 and the Colt instead of the Python. Both pistols would be good choices, but I'm partial to the 1911 myself." I ran my hand along the bottom of the bag, and saw him tense up a split second before my hand felt something lying flat on the bottom. I pulled it out to find a thick sheaf of bearer bonds and three plastic coin sheets full of round one ounce silver and gold bullion. I tossed the bearer bonds but gave him an approving nod as I held up the bullion before putting it back in the bag. I gestured for him to follow me, and headed for where I knew his office was.

"I figured the .45 carried more bullets," he said as we went down the hallway.

"It does, and it's just as reliable as the Python. Do you still have that .22 rifle you got Amy?"

"Of course! I spent almost five hundred dollars on the damn thing. And Amy wouldn't let me sell it anyway."

"Let's get it, and all the ammo you have for it," I said as we stepped through the door to his office. He had his big desk facing the side wall, with his gun safe on the opposite side of the room, next to a shelf that displayed copies of certificates and awards that were useless now.

"It's just a little .22," he said dismissively while he opened the safe and drew out a Ruger 10/22 with a pink stock and foregrip. It sported a scope that looked like a little four power job, and a sling in pink leather. "And…it's pink." He handed it to me and turned to collect the boxes of ammunition as I dropped the magazine and pulled the bolt back to check the chamber. When I looked up, he was frowning at me.

"You're as bad as Maya," he grumbled. "I know how to take care of a gun, god damn it."

"Karl, I do this with every gun I pick up. It's a habit, not a judgment. Rule Fifteen: Assume every gun is loaded if you're not in a fight, and never point a gun at anything you want to keep. I assumed you did it with your own guns." He raised an eyebrow at that.

"How many rules do you have?" he asked as he put the boxes of ammunition on the desk and pulled out a canvas gun case.

"Twenty two for survival. I never bothered to count the personal rules." I reached for one of the boxes. The Ruger 10/22 had a ten round rotary magazine, and I started thumbing rounds into it.

"Which one helps you survive Maya?" he asked.

"I choose my conflicts very carefully," I said after I finished loading the magazine. "Got any more magazines for this?" He nodded and handed me two more of the boxy little ten round mags.

"That's it?" Karl said incredulously. I looked up from what I was doing and gave him an enigmatic smirk.

"I know the difference between opinion and fact, Karl. And I never argue over an opinion." He looked at me like I'd just spoken to him in Swahili, and I went back to the task at hand. He grabbed the other magazine and started loading it. When we were done he laid the magazine on the desk. I slipped one of the loaded magazines into the rifle and laid it on the desk.

"Why did you pick Amy up early, Karl? Did you know what was going on today?" I watched his face for some kind of reaction, but all I got was a disappointed half-grimace as he shook his head.

"No, I was having lunch with a client, a member of the school board, when he got a call. Next thing I knew, he was half-way to the door. When I said something to him, he told me to go pick Amy up right then. I'm glad I listened."

"Next order of business: maps. Do you still keep a current Springfield map on hand for work?" I got a look of pure "Duh!" for that, and he pulled one from the top of the gun safe.

"Do insurance companies hate paying out on policies?" he said with a tone that made it sound like I should already know how obvious the answer was.

"When we go back in there, you need to be the one to give Amy this," I said as I handed him the pink rifle.

"Why?" he said, instantly suspicious.

"One because you bought it for her in the first place, plus it's your job as her father to make sure she uses it responsibly. And, there's no way in Hell I would ever hand her a pink gun." He held up a hand in mock surrender.

"Seemed like a good idea at the time. And she was twelve. She still wanted to be a princess." We shared a brief laugh at that, since both of us remembered Amy at that age. It seemed like a good note to head back on, so I headed out of the office.

When we made it back into the dining room, we found that Amy and Maya had been busy while we were gone. Porsche's P-A duffel bag was lying empty on the table, and she was stuffing things into the backpack Amy's bug-out bag had originally been in. Amy's camping backpack was stuffed full, and her own duffel bag was empty, too. Meanwhile, Maya had finished stripping the commercial first aid kit and was putting the lid back on the clear plastic container. Her bug out bag and purse were next to it, and the big blue tub was sealed and ready to go as well. Sherman got up from where he was laying by the front door and ambled into the dining room to sit beside me.

"Okay, folks," I said before anyone else could open their mouth. "I want at least two people to a vehicle. Maya, we're going to have to leave your car behind. You'll ride shotgun, literally, with Karl and Amy in his Range Rover." Both of them protested loudly at that until I laid the spare pistol down on the table in front of Maya.

"Dave, it'll be like World War Three with them in the same car," Amy said. "Well, it's true," she told them off their looks.

"It won't," I said calmly. "In case anyone has missed the memo, the world is ending outside those doors. If we're going to stay alive, you are going to have to work together. Our primary goal is survival. Nothing else matters but that. Karl, you're driving. Maya, if anything needs shooting, you shoot it. Twice. Amy, your eyes need to be where your mom or dad aren't looking. Our destination is our house. If we get separated, just make sure you end up there. Any questions?"

"Can I ride with you?" Amy asked me.

"No," I answered flatly. "Maya calls the shots in the Range Rover. If she says do something, you do it."

"It's my truck, I think I should be the one in charge," Karl said. I could see his chest puffing out as he got ready to assert himself.

80

"Maya is my partner, Karl. She knows the plan, where to go and what to do. You don't. You and your truck are worthless without her on board. End of story."

"No, it isn't," he said. "It's your plan, but it's my vehicle and my daughter. And I'm in charge in my vehicle. You're going to have to deal with that." He stepped forward again and tried the looming trick again. It still didn't work.

"If your daughter's survival takes a back seat to your pride, then you have no business coming with us anyway. You need to decide, right now, which one is more important to you, because we can survive without you." I watched him to see which side of his brain he listened to. His lips pursed together, then he seemed to draw in on himself.

"Amy is the most important thing in the world to me," he said after a few seconds. "I'll listen to Maya."

"I knew you wouldn't let her down. Let's get loaded up and hit the road." I led everyone out the back door, and found Sherman trotting at my side. It only took us a minute to load the tubs up into the back of Karl's truck. Personal bags were tossed on top of them, then I went to the bikes and started pulling them down. Porsche and Maya were at my side, pulling the other two down before I could ask for help, and we wheeled them out to Karl's Range Rover. Maya knew what I was up to, but I wasn't sure why Porsche had decided to pitch in. Still, it was a gift horse whose dentistry I wasn't examining. Maya trotted back to the garage while I secured the bikes to the rack on the rear bumper, and came back with a pull behind child-carrier.

"You are brilliant," I said softly as I jumped down to help her heft it into the back of his truck. We worked as quietly as we could, with no idea of when the infected would make their way here. Once everything was secure, we made our way to the side door of the garage.

"We're ready," Karl said with an edge of uncertainty to his voice. "We just need to move Maya's car out of the driveway, and we can go."

"Do you have everything from your car that you want, baby?" I asked her.

"It'll just take me a few seconds to grab what I need to," she said. I gave her a nod, and she walked to the door.

"We'll go when you start your car. Amy, Karl, mount up. I'll open the garage door." My pulse started hammering in my ears as I sent Porsche to her truck. Sherman hopped in the back seat with Amy while Karl got behind the wheel. It was time to get moving. So help me, I was looking forward to getting back out there.

Chapter 8

Side Trips

Adversity makes men, and prosperity makes monsters.

~ Victor Hugo ~

By the time we made it to Sunshine Street, I was starting to feel the tension of the last half hour in my shoulders. We'd wound through the back streets and managed to avoid contact with any infected by going slowly and avoiding main roads. I still shuddered at the memory of the screams we heard from the Unity Church that we had passed, and shoved it to the back of my mind. I had worries enough in front of me. Sunshine wasn't as badly congested as I'd feared, but it was crawling, in some places literally, with infected. Most of them were heading east in groups, probably heading toward the sounds of gunshots, screams and car horns that came from that direction. We were lurking in the shadows of a side street, out of easy sight from Sunshine.

"Well, there aren't any cars, but I don't know how we're going to get past the cannibalistic undead traffic jam," I whispered to Porsche.

"Maybe we can outrun them," she said. I hunkered down in the truck bed and flashed my penlight at the map, but nothing had changed since the last time I'd looked at it. The two streets that were the closest to us on the other side of the road were dead ends, and the only street that went through was several blocks to the east. There was no way we would make it that far without being overwhelmed by hungry dead people. I tried starting from the other end, thinking I'd need to get to Barnes Street and trying to find a connecting point from there and something caught my eye. I traced my finger along the map until I was sure and looked up with a smile.

"Porsche, I am fucking brilliant," I said.

"Humble, too. What did you find?"

"The quickest way north. No traffic, no people."

"No zombies?"

"No zombies. I'll be right back." I slid over the side of the bed and froze when I saw a zombie stop along the road. It looked in my direction for a few moments, and I fought to keep from moving as my lizard brain tried to tell me to shoot it or run. The smarter part of me, though, urged me to keep still. It was dark where I was, and the zombie probably couldn't see me. If I made a sudden move, though, it might see the movement or hear me, and if that happened, the chain of events that followed would bring more of them down this dark little road, and that meant more running and shooting and maybe a lot of screaming. After a few seconds, it turned its head back and started shambling forward, and I let out the breath I'd been holding.

Karl rolled his window down as I approached the Range Rover. I put my finger to my lips as I got closer to forestall any questions. It worked like Plan A usually did.

"What are you waiting for?" he asked in his usual courtroom baritone. I froze and looked back over my shoulder, but the street was clear for the moment.

"I'm waiting for you to make enough noise to call every zombie in the area right down on us," I said angrily. "Sunshine is hopeless here, but I found a way across east of here. Follow us. And get ready to go. Once we kick this off, there won't be much time for turning around or asking questions."

"What way?" he asked as I turned and headed back to the truck. I didn't bother with walking slowly or even covering the noise I made.

"When you see the next zombie herd pass, turn on your lights and honk your horn," I said when I reached the side of Porsche's truck.

"That'll bring every one of the damn things for a square mile!" Porsche cried out.

"Yeah, that's the plan," I told her as I clambered into the truck bed. Behind us, the Range Rover's transmission whined as

Karl backed it up. Then it changed pitch as he turned, shifted and pulled around, presumably facing the other way. In front of us, a group of undead in business suits and skirts shambled into sight, and Porsche hit the lights. Her horn warbled for a few seconds before it died, and I heard her cursing.

"Go! GO!" I yelled as they turned to face us in slow, chilling unison. Tires squealed as she hit the gas, and we were flying away from the street in reverse. I braced myself against the open window and held on for dear life, literally. We flew past the Range Rover, and I felt the truck lurch to the right, then rubber was screeching as the truck spun through a one-eighty plus a few degrees before it came to a stop. She dropped it into drive and sped back down the street.

"I hope you know what the hell you're doing!" she yelled back at me.

"Me, too!" I said. "That was terrific! Where did you learn to drive like that?"

"I didn't mean to do that. I was just trying to pull into a driveway and turn around!" I laughed and looked back over my shoulder. The Range Rover was behind us, and behind *it* was a crowd of very hungry infected.

"Well, it worked! Just don't ever do that again! At least, not with me in the back of the truck. I almost ended up in someone's front yard. Now, slow down and take the left!"

"Yeah, sorry about that," she lied as she coasted through the turn.

"No you aren't. Second left and…take the first right after that. That should put us on Langston Street." She took the turns, and I directed her to take the next left after that, onto a little street called Luster. The neighborhood looked like a hold out from the Sixties or Seventies, with little ranch style brick and siding houses. I looked back over my shoulder as we passed under the first street light to see the Rover turning onto the street behind us, minus the undead horde. I breathed a sigh of relief at that.

"Right on the last street, that should be…Washita. Take it down to the end, then dog leg left across Lone Pine."

"All of those streets are dead ends or cul-de-sacs!" she said.

"Trust me, I know what I'm doing," I said. She shook her head and made the right turn. Street lights passed overhead as we sped down the street, then we were making the thirty yard run to the left turn. A trio of street lights shone on a row of upscale houses that sported open garage doors and dark windows.

"This place feels creepy," Porsche said.

"We take Amy down this street every year when we go looking at Christmas lights," I said. "It's her favorite place, because every house is lit up."

"It's also a dead end," Porsche shot back.

"Not exactly. Go down that driveway there, the one that runs by the house at the end." She pulled into the driveway slowly. Her headlights lit up the concrete path, and showed the curve where it led behind the house. Cement ended just beyond the trees that shielded the residents from the view of the squat metal shed with the Union Pacific logo on it, and a dirt road led further into the darkness.

"I never knew this was here!" Porsche said.

"We needed a path across Sunshine. I give you the Union Pacific railroad. No cars, no people and zero zombies."

"You are fucking brilliant, Dave!" she crowed as the road led onto the rocky easement that ran along either side of the railroad track. The Range Rover scraped the trees on one side, then lumbered out behind us.

"And humble," I said. She turned toward Sunshine and hit the gas. The ride was bumpy as hell, but it was a hell of a lot faster, and it beat trying to dodge the infected. A bank came into view on our left as the trees on that side ended after a few yards. The truck slowed, but I couldn't see any dead walking around. "Go, while the coast is clear. And get on the other side of the tracks at the crossing." She nodded and hit the gas again. For a few brief seconds, my teeth weren't trying to rattle out of my head as we hit asphalt. On my right, I saw the Domino's Pizza sign, and wished for a slice of pepperoni pizza so bad I could almost taste it. Porsche cut across the road at an angle, and we hit dirt again all too soon. The Range Rover followed a second later, and Karl negotiated the crossing just as smoothly. Trees loomed on either side of us as we bounced along.

"I think you should turn your headlights on now," I told Porsche. The ground in front of us lit up, and the truck picked up speed. Gravel crunched beneath our wheels, drowning out most of the sounds of horror around us. For several minutes, the only thing we had to worry about was the tracks splitting for a few hundred yards and making the easement narrower. That, and whether or not I was going to lose any fillings. Finally, I saw the familiar white light from one of the electrical boxes at some crossings. I asked Porsche to stop a little ways before we got to the crossing, and the truck slowed to a gradual halt. When Karl stopped behind us, I hopped out of the bed and went to the passenger window. Maya leaned her head out as I walked up. In the back seat, Amy looked at me with worried eyes. Karl was rolling his window back up and doing his level best not to look peeved at not being consulted directly.

"Everything okay?" Maya asked.

"Yeah, we're good," I said as I leaned against her door. "I need to go take care of my end of something. We're not far from home, and you should be able to make it there okay from here. Head to the house and get everything ready for the run to Sherwood. I figure we'll have power for a little longer, so try to get our Kindles charged. Plan on sheltering in place for another day or two, just in case." She leaned out and kissed me.

"I know the drill baby," she said softly. "We'll be ready to go by the time you get back."

"I know. I'm just…worried. Nothing's gone the way it was supposed to, and I get the feeling that it's going to get a lot worse before we get out of town."

"It's the zombie apocalypse honey. I'm pretty sure nothing's going the way it should," she said with that pragmatic, dry tone that I'd never gotten tired of hearing. I felt a smile cross my face, probably the first genuine one I'd had all day.

"And *that* is why I love you," I told her. I kissed her and stepped back. "I'll be there as soon as I can."

"Be careful, Dave!" Amy called out from the back seat. I turned back and gave her a thumb's up before I went to the passenger side of Porsche's Nissan.

"What's going on?" she asked when I slid into the seat.

"We're splitting up here. You and I are going to pick up someone else. Maya's going home to get things ready to bug out. Stay on the railroad tracks until we get to the next crossing, then follow the road to the right. It should be Barnes Street." She put the truck in gear and pulled forward. We rolled across the grass and back onto asphalt, and I checked the road on my side. It looked pretty clear. Karl pulled forward and turned down the road, and Porsche drove over the low curb and back onto the grass.

"So, who are we going to get, and why are they so important?" Porsche asked when we were bumping along on the rough ground beside the tracks again.

"Remember the guys I was telling you about at work?"

"The ones from Iraq?" she said.

"Yeah. One of them, Nate Reid, is a former Delta Force operator. He's the one who made me believe that something like this was going to happen. He also helped me get ready for it if…*when* it did. He helped me finance Sherwood, our property out west of town, and made sure I got everything I needed to ride things out. In return, he asked me to make sure I got his ex-wife and his son to safety when shit hit the fan."

"Why you?"

"His son likes the War of the Magi series."

"You're kidding," she laughed.

"He's got signed copies of all three books. And they're pretty damn good. Hell, they're better than Operation Terror and The Frankenstein Code."

"No, I meant that he chose you just because his son liked your books."

"There's more to it than that, but that's what started everything. Now, if you'll excuse me, I need to call Cassie and let her know we're on our way." I pulled my phone out of my pocket and prayed for a signal. I got a couple of bars. It wasn't much, but it was enough. Her phone rang several times, and just when I thought it was going to go to voicemail, she picked up.

"Hello?" she said softly.

"Cassie, it's Dave Stewart. Are you at home?" I heard the phone rub against fabric, then her voice came clearer.

"If this is really you, what did you tell my son when he bought Operation Terror?" she asked.

"You didn't let him read that one, or The Frankenstein Code."

"Damn straight," she said. "I read them, but only you would know that I didn't let Bryce see them. Nate called me a few hours ago, he told me to expect you. Come on by. We'll be waiting for you." The phone clicked off and I tucked it back in my front pocket.

"That was quick. And weird. What was that about your books?" Porsche asked.

"She was making sure it was really me," I said absently. "Nate had already called her. There, take that road. Follow it down to Grand. No, wait!"

"What?"

"Stay on the tracks. This street comes out between two churches. Stay on the tracks until they cross Grand."

"Yeah, we don't want to run up on another prayer meeting from Hell," she agreed. We endured another ten minutes of rough terrain before we came out on Grand. The little hill that rose up to meet the tracks shielded us from view to the west, and I saw a group of infected milling around under the street light a few hundred yards to the east, right where the two churches sat caddy-corner to each other. It made an irrational sense that we'd find more zombies there. People gravitated to churches when things went bad, and right now, it was as bad as it got. There was a sort of comfort to be found in seeking the presence of God, and even if I had very little good to say about *religion*, I understood the human need for the spiritual. Even in death, people could find comfort in that, perhaps especially in death. Maybe they were already in a better place. Even if they were, I was in no hurry to join them.

Porsche turned her lights off again and let the truck idle. None of them seemed to be heading our way, so I gave her a nod and pointed to the little street a few yards to our right. Three turns later, we were pulling up in front of Cassie's place. Her street was comfortably cute, with well-kept lawns and minivans in every other driveway. Cassie's was one of the ones without the minivan or the prerequisite garden sculptures. We pulled into the driveway of her place and got out. We walked up to the door and I knocked softly, half expecting to be met with a gun barrel in my face.

"It's open Dave," I heard her call out. I turned the knob and pushed the door open but stayed in place. Carefully, I slung the M4 barrel down across my shoulder.

"Cassie, it's me. I have someone with me, her name's Porsche. She's a friend of mine. She's okay." I stepped inside and kept my hands out to my sides, knowing I was silhouetted against the open door. The broad side of most barns would be harder to hit than I was just then. Porsche followed me in with her hands held up in front of her, and I heard the door swing shut behind us.

"Sorry for being paranoid, Dave," Cassie said from behind me.

"It's been that kind of day," I told her as I turned around.

"Nate was pretty insistent about being careful." Cassie was holding a Berretta M9 of her own pointed down at the floor. In the soft light from the street light, the only other thing I could see were her jeans and hiking boots.

"It was a good idea. I've already had to shoot at a couple of survivors. You ready?"

"We were just getting packed to go." She stepped forward, and I could see that she had on a gray sweater and had her blond hair pulled into a messy ponytail. She led us into the dining room table. A half-full backpack and gear covered the table. "I sort of... unpacked the bug out bags. I kept all of the stuff, but it felt weird having all of it packed up." I shrugged. Movement behind me caught my attention, and I saw Bryce emerge from the hallway with a backpack in his hand. His face lit up when he saw us.

"Hi, Dave!" he said brightly as he came over to us and dropped the pack at Cassie's feet. "Dad said you'd be coming by." He'd grown a couple of inches since I'd last seen him, and his dark hair had grown out from the buzz he'd had six months ago. Now it was in danger of getting in his eyes. He wore a pair of jeans and an Iron Man t-shirt with a pair of black sneakers. His face was just starting to lose the soft edges of baby fat, and his chin and jaw were looking more like Nate's square features. His nose, though, was pure Cassie, slightly upturned and freckled.

"You ready to go, then?" I asked as he shook my hand.

"Just about. I didn't unpack my stuff," he said with a smile. For a kid, I figured having a pack full of gear was pretty novel. "All I had to do was pack my clothes." He turned a smug look on his mother and got a glare that I could feel the heat off of from across the room in return.

"Enough of that, young man," she said sternly as she put the last of her gear into the pack. He nodded and gave me a knowing smile while she shouldered her pack and grabbed her purse. "Go get in the car."

"Mom, what about my gun?" he asked plaintively. He was bordering on whining, and I would have been too at his age. I gave her a nod, and she let out a tired sigh and headed back toward the hallway. She emerged moments later with a black rectangular gun case in her hand and a stern expression on her face.

"You are not opening this until we get to Dave's house, do you understand me young man?" she said. His face lit up as she handed him the case, and he headed for the garage door. "We'll meet you outside," she told me as she followed him. Porsche hit the door a heartbeat before I did, then stopped in her tracks on the welcome mat. My ears perked up as I tried to keep from running into her, and I heard the sound of metal hitting metal nearby. Before either of us could say anything, the distinctive hammering of a machine gun ripped across the night. Without thinking, I went to push Porsche forward but she was already moving toward her truck. Two steps behind her, I unslung the M4 and vaulted into the bed even as the garage door started to open. She had her truck started and in reverse before the door was halfway up, and by the time it had cleared the roof of Cassie's grey Wrangler, we were in the street. I looked to my left to see a black Humvee barrel through the next intersection over, followed seconds later by another. The second one was the source of the gunfire, the man in the turret hosing the road behind them with a steady stream of fire.

The machine gun stopped a heartbeat or three later, and I heard the sound of men calling out to each other. For a moment, I might as well have been back in Iraq, listening to an infantry squad. There is always an urgency to combat, but the men I had heard over in the sand box had a distinctive focus to their voices in a fight, a cadence unique to American fighting men. Hearing it now, in the States, I couldn't change how I reacted.

"Left! Left!" I called out.

"Are you nuts? There's zombies that way!" Porsche cried.

"Don't argue with me! Go left!" I yelled back. She cursed a blue streak, but she turned the wheel to the left and left rubber smoking in our wake as we barreled down the street.

"Which way do I turn?" she yelled back through the window as we sped toward the intersection.

"Right!" I called back as I braced myself for the turn.

"I should've known," she said as she turned the wheel. The street slid into view in front of us, and I saw a Humvee turned on its side with several men crawling out of it. Two were on either end of the vehicle, and a third was crawling out of the turret. Porsche pulled up next to the Humvee and stopped. Through her windshield, I could see a group of infected coming down the street, moving too fast to be zombies. Even as I got to my feet, the soldier on the far end of the Humvee dropped one of them with a short burst to the chest. The other one pointed his gun at me. I forced myself to ignore the thick stubby barrel that was pointed at me and propped my elbows on the roof to steady my aim, then popped off a three round burst into the chest of one of the infected. The sweats-and-hoodie clad ghoul dropped, and I moved my aim to the right. Three more rounds peppered the torso of a naked ghoul, and I thanked whichever god happened to be listening for bad lighting and the fog of war as he fell.

"Get in!" I yelled between bursts.

"You heard the man, get in! Mason, talk to me!" the man who had pointed his gun at me called out. His gun hiccupped and another ghoul went down. I fired a stuttering burst from the M4, but mine spun and staggered but stayed on his feet. I squeezed off another three rounds, and he fell. *Twelve rounds,* I reminded myself.

"Kowalski and Hicks are dead, Renfro took a round in the right arm!" someone called from inside the Humvee. In my peripheral vision, I could see men crawling out of the Humvee.

"Jackson, get Renfro out," the leader barked out. He put three rounds downrange, then another three. "Mason, Vasquez, pull the gear. Carter, grab the SINGCARS and get ready to pop thermite. You, in the truck…keep shooting those fuckers!"

"I've only got a couple more magazines!" I called back over the ringing in my ears. I switched the selector to single fire.

"Use 'em!" he yelled back as soldiers crawled out of the vehicle. Porsche's door opened and I saw her prop her arm against the frame. The pop of her pistol was a slow counter beat to the ping of my M4. I spared a glance at the leader, and saw him struggling with the turret as I felt the bed of the truck vibrate under my feet. Then a soldier was beside me, and my gun went silent. As I fished a magazine from my pocket, he opened up with his submachine gun, three round bursts coughing from the end of the barrel. Ghouls dropped as I rammed the magazine home and pulled the charging handle. Porsche's gun went silent and I heard her curse.

"Get in!" I yelled to her, taking aim at a ghoul in a business skirt that was sprinting along the sidewalk on my left. I let the sight go past her slightly before I pulled the trigger, but she kept going. Another aimed shot missed her, so I brought the scope back onto her and started pulling the trigger as I slowly walked it ahead of her. The fifth round dropped her, and I turned back to the advancing horde. Seven more rounds dropped four infected ghouls, and then the leader stepped out in front of the truck with a boxy gun in hand. The guy beside me slapped my shoulder with the back of his left hand.

"Hold your fire!" he yelled. I raised the barrel of my gun and nodded as he called out again. "Put 'em down, Captain!" In front of the truck, the captain raised the bulkier gun to his shoulder and unleashed a brand of hell on Earth on the ghouls that I was glad I was on the back side of. The sound of it alone hammered my ears, a deeper pounding than the M4's sharp reports, and I saw the top half of one of the ghouls jerk uncontrollably before its head disintegrated. The captain lowered the barrel and slowly walked a line of destruction across the advancing line, sending body parts flying, including at least one arm and a head. A few seconds later, the gun clicked as the last round cycled through it, and very few of the ghouls were left standing. The man beside me let out a whoop as the captain turned and walked back to the truck.

"Fuck yeah!" one of the other soldiers called out.

"Stow that shit, Jackson," the captain said as he climbed into the bed of the truck and laid the big gun down. He nodded to one of the other soldiers, a young black man who still stood by the truck. The soldier ran to the Humvee and pulled the pin on a grenade, laid it on the upper side of the vehicle then bolted for the truck again. Porsche didn't need to be told to gun the engine, and we sped past the damaged vehicle as the thermite ignited. Cassie sped along behind us, and I heard the diesel catch as we turned the corner. I leaned down by the open driver's side window.

"Head back to where we split up," I told Porsche. She nodded, her face slowly losing a slight green cast in the fitful light.

"Thanks for the ride!" the captain said to me as Porsche made her way back toward the railroad tracks. He stuck out one gloved hand. "Name's Adams."

"Stewart," I said. "Dave Stewart. What the hell happened back there?" Adams gave a glance to one of his men before he turned back to me.

"Fuckin' Homeland pukes rammed us when we hit that big bunch of infected," he said. Even over the ringing in my ears and the wind, I could hear the scorn in his voice. "Opened fire with my team down range, too. Killed two of my men. Did you say your name was Dave Stewart?"

"Yeah," I said.

"You the guy who wrote The Frankenstein Code?" the guy beside me asked.

"Yeah, and Operation Terror." He gave a nod to Adams.

"I read your stuff, man. Not bad. Kinda out there, but hey, it's just a horror story, right?"

"Not anymore," I said.

Chapter 9

A Little Knowledge

*Great achievement is usually born of great sacrifice, and
is never the result of selfishness.*

~Napoleon Hill ~

"Garland, this is Karma," Adams said into his radio as we
bounced along the right of way beside the tracks. One earphone
was held to his ear, the other swinging from the curved headset
to bounce against his shoulder. "Tertiary objective sighted.
Preparing to secure. We are down two KIA, one wounded." He
listened to the response on his headphones, then looked over his
shoulder at Cassie's Jeep. "Negative on secondary objective.
Homeland rabbited on us before we could verify that intel. Roger
that." He kept the headphone to his ear and looked back toward
the front of the truck with the impatient expression of a man on
hold.

"Hey, Stewart," the man beside me asked. His name tape
read Vasquez. He pointed to the carbine in my hand before he
went on. "Where'd you pick up the M4?"

"Ran across a couple of National Guard trucks outside
Kickapoo," I said as I reached into my right front pocket.
"Grabbed what I needed to stay alive, and pulled their tags. I
figured someone should know what happened to them." I handed
him the three sets of tags.

"What did happen to them?" he said, and I heard a little
hostility creep into his voice.

"Near as I can figure, they tried to clear a bunch of infected
from the high school and got overrun." I watched his face, and
saw the look change from hostile to skeptical as he looked down
at the tags in his hand.

"They turned?" he asked.

"Yeah. I took care of them, and we led as many infected
away as we could," I told him. He gave me a nod, then turned to
Adams. In their gear and helmets, they had that lean uniformity

97

that I'd seen in so many front-line soldiers. They wore smaller helmets but their other gear was not much different from most I'd seen: tactical vests and holsters, elbow and knee pads and heavy gloves over digital camo fatigues. Their shoulder patches bore the Special Forces tab, most of them having a Ranger tab above the obligatory Airborne tab. All of them bore the subdued version of the Special Forces shoulder patches, an upright sword crossed by three lightning bolts in black against the olive drab arrowhead. I reassessed my situation as I realized that I was sitting among a team of Green Berets, men who had earned the term 'bad-ass' several times over before they'd even made the grade for the Special Forces. If there was a place that could be called safe in the newly fucked up world, I was as close to it as humanly possible.

"Negative," Adams said suddenly. "I repeat, negative sir. Infected are one thing, but that is an order I will not follow. Yes, sir, I understand who it comes from, and that does not make it a lawful order. No, sir. Understood sir." He threw the headphones down and spat something I couldn't hear, but suspected it was something unpleasant. The graveled roadway rose to meet the concrete bed of Bennett St., and Porsche turned the truck's nose east. Cassie pulled up behind her, her Jeep idling easily.

"What's the plan Captain?" Carter asked from his place next to the tailgate.

"We secure the secondary and tertiary objectives, then head back to base." The soldier across from me looked back toward Cassie's truck, nothing more than a shifting of his eyes, and his face seemed to cloud. "Maximum discretion, people." Without another word, all but Vasquez and Adams grabbed gear before they got out of the bed of the truck and spread out a little, two on each side, one facing forward, the other to the rear. In the dim light, I could barely make out Adams' expression as he turned toward me, putting his face in shadow. Something in my gut tightened, an instinct that I'd learned to listen to in the past few hours.

"Mister Stewart, thank you for the ride," Adams said as Vasquez turned toward me but made no move to get out of the truck. "We certainly owe you our lives." In the instant before he moved, his stance changed, something I probably would have missed if I wasn't already expecting something to go wrong. Without a second thought, I grabbed his vest and pushed myself backward, pushing Vasquez out of the bed of the truck along with me. I landed on Vasquez, and Adams landed on me.

"Porsche! Go!" I yelled. I heard Cassie gun the engine on her Jeep, and Porsche hit the gas, sending her truck forward in a screech of burning rubber. Cassie's Jeep shot past a split second later, and I could hear the pounding of boots and cursing around us. The dwindling red dots of their tail-lights down Bennett was almost as rewarding as being with them. Cassie knew the way to my house, and Porsche was smart enough to follow her lead. I had kept my end of the bargain, and Nate would keep his. Maya and Amy had a shot at surviving.

Adams pulled me to my feet with a curse. "You son of a bitch!" he snarled in my face.

"Sorry I screwed up your snatch and grab," I said as a strange sort of elation bubbled up inside me. Even if they killed me right there, I'd already won. My girls were safe, my friend was safe and so was Nate's family. Somehow, though, I didn't think Adams was likely to do that. He was a Green Beret, a consummate professional. His trade might have been war, but somehow, I knew that he wouldn't kill me in cold blood. He shook me once, then pushed me away. I staggered back, barely keeping my feet. Then he was turning back toward me, and I barely registered his fist moving before it slammed into my jaw. *So,* I thought as my face plummeted toward the concrete, *I guess hitting me is still an option.*

I came to with a headache and a throbbing in my jaw that made dropping back into oblivion pretty damn inviting. My shoulders ached and something was digging into my wrists, probably the same something that was holding them behind my back. I opened my eyes to find myself in a cage, stripped down to my boxers. Around me I could see bleachers and scoreboards, as my senses slowly told me I was in a basketball court. To my left I could see a set of tables covered with boxes and cables, and in front of me stood black clad men with assault rifles held at the ready, barrels down and fingers outside the trigger guards. They didn't have the look of soldiers, and a couple had goatees and hair longer than military regs allowed sticking out from under their ball caps. A dry, rasping laugh came from my right, and I turned to see a man strapped to an angled table that held him almost upright in the cell next to mine. Only bars separated us, and some part of me didn't think that was enough. As my eyes focused on him, I changed my guess. He might have been a man once, but whatever he was now, 'man' wasn't the right word for it. His eyes were milky white, and his skin had the gray pallor of death. His face was gaunt, exposing every line of the skull beneath it, and the few clumps of hair on his scalp looked like they had faded to a dull gray. I admit it, I stared at him, and some part of my brain sort of locked up as it tried to force what I was seeing to make sense. Then it turned its head and looked straight at me.

Oh yeah, my brain suddenly told itself, *zombies*.

"What the hell are you lookin' at, asshole?" the thing asked. Its voice was a raspy parody of human speech, but it was at least understandable. "You eyeballin' me?"

"Kinda hard not to," I said with an instinctive animosity. The urge to kill this thing was growing in the back of my thoughts, and I had no idea why. Even if I did know why, I didn't care. All that mattered was that this thing ended up dead. The world would be a better place without the thing in the next cell in it, of that I was certain.

"I'm gonna fuck you up when I get out of here," the thing said to me. That pissed me off even more, and I felt my lips curl back from my teeth. My heart started pounding as I gave him a cold glare.

"That's something I'd like to see you pull off," another voice intruded. I turned to the front of my cage to see Captain Adams standing next to a man in black fatigues and a baseball cap. His clothes were unmarred by any insignia, and he wore a massive handgun in a tactical holster on his right thigh. The chrome slide contrasted with the black grips, and by the shape of the slde, I guessed he was carrying a Desert Eagle of some caliber or another. "You know, I was surprised that this little shit stain of a city rated three targets. And here we have two of them.

"Who are you?" I asked.

"The man asking the questions, Mr. Stewart. That's all you need to know. You can call me 'Sir' if you need to address me by some kind of name."

"Sure thing asshole," I said. Adams suppressed a laugh, but a snort still got through.

"Let's start with the basics. How long have you been colluding with Nathan Reid?" he asked. Adams face went blank at that, and I decided to test a theory.

"Captain Reid helped me with a couple of my books. That's common knowledge to anyone who read them," I answered casually. Blackshirt's eyes narrowed and I could see his jaw clench, while Adams' mouth quirked a little, like he was trying to hide a smile. His eyes flicked to Blackshirt for a moment, and the grin started to form.

"Don't try to bullshit me, Stewart. You attacked the men sent to retrieve you, you knew we were after you, and because of you, a pair of fugitives are running loose in this city. Now, stop playing games with me. Where is Reid?"

"A mother and her kid are fugitives? What did they do? Skip a PTA meeting or something?"

"Where is he?"

"No idea," I answered.

"We know you were in contact with him today. We have your phone. Tell me what I want to know, or I'll have you stripped naked and thrown outside the wall."

"I've been out in the shit all night, and I started with next to nothing," I said. "Come back when you can make a real threat." From my right came the wheezing laughter I'd heard earlier.

"How about I come in there and work your god damn kneecaps over with a ballpeen hammer?" he said with an impotent snarl. "How's that for a threat?"

"Come on in," I said. "I'd hold the door for you, but I'm kind of tied up right now." His eyes went to the door, then back to me. Behind him, Adams shook his head.

"Talk to me or I'll find your girlfriend and splatter her brains on the wall while you watch. Maybe we'll do her little girl, too. She'll die screaming for you to help her." My eyes narrowed as he said that. They didn't need my phone. They had been monitoring it all day. My conversation with Amy hadn't been in my texts, but he knew she looked to me for help. The animosity I'd been feeling for the thing in the cell next to me had no trouble switching targets.

"Give it up, Keyes," Adams said. "He's getting more intel out of you than you're getting out of him."

"Fuck you, Adams," Keyes said. "When you have my permission to have an opinion, I'll tell you what it is in a memo. I'll conduct my interrogations any way I see fit."

"Tell him," Adams said to me.

"You're afraid to come into these cells. You've been monitoring my cell phone all day. The walking cadaver over there is your primary target, Nate Reid's family is the secondary, and I'm the tertiary target because of my association with them. That tells me that you think he knows something, and that you need leverage on him to keep him quiet or under control, which tells me you're probably to blame for the zombie clusterfuck going on out there or you know who is. You're carrying a chromed Desert Eagle on your hip instead of a Sig Sauer or a Browning, so you're not military, and I'm pretty sure you're not even really government. That makes you either a mercenary or private security with a tendency to over-compensate. Did I miss anything?" I asked Adams. He turned to Keyes, who gave him a glare and stalked out of the room.

"Your story checked out," Adams said after a door slammed nearby. "The detachment at Kickapoo reported a Nissan truck showing up and drawing the bulk of the infected away from the front barrier before they evac'd."

"Don't expect me to roll over now that you're going all good-cop on me," I said. Adams shrugged.

"Whatever Keyes wants to know, he can get on his own. I don't know who he really works for, but it sure as hell ain't Homeland Security. What I do know is that I served with Nate Reid when we were both Rangers, back in oh-four. He's a good man, and any man he trusts his family with is okay in my book. My team is on the next chopper out of here. I just wanted to say thanks for the help. And sorry about punching you."

"You were doing your job, man," I shrugged. "You have one hell of a right hook."

"Aw, isn't that sweet," the thing in the cage next to me croaked. "You two got a regular little bro-mance goin' on."

"What the hell is that thing, anyway?" I asked, tilting my head toward the next cell.

"Mike Deacon, Springfield's version of Patient Zero. First case reported. At first they thought it was some guy on bathsalts or something like that. Got arrested after he tore his girlfriend's throat out with his teeth. Best guess is he's the primary carrier, and she woke up in the morgue at St John's, then infected the rest of the city through the people she attacked. This shit spread's so damn quick, though, it's hard to say what really happened."

"But he can still talk...and think?" I asked.

"Yeah, ain't that fucked up?" Adams said. I looked back over at Deacon, and fought the urge to try to kill him. "He's the tenth one we've captured. The folks at the CDC figure every city has one."

"Where did he get it from?" I asked as I turned back to Adams. He gave me a perplexed look, and opened his mouth to say something. A second later, he closed it, then looked back at Deacon. The living zombie started to laugh again as a door opened off to my left.

103

"Captain Adams!" a soldier in full combat gear called out with a note of panic in his voice. "They're hitting the fences!" From outside, the harsh buzz of a klaxon sounded, and I heard a tinny voice calling for all personnel to report to their posts. Adams cursed and sprinted for the door, unslinging his M4 as he went. He gestured to two of the men standing guard and told them to stay put, and the rest followed him to the door.

"Adams!" I called out. He turned at the door and looked back at me. "Where the hell are we?"

"Missouri State University!" he said, then bolted out.

"You're about to die, and you ask where you are?" Deacon asked. "You should have asked him to let you out. You would have lived a little longer." He looked down at the straps that held him down and flexed his arm. There was a groaning sound as metal strained against the force applied to it, and the two guards stepped forward, gun butts to their shoulders.

"I have that covered," I told him. My fingers curled up and I touched the bonds on my wrist. A narrow plastic band encircled my wrists, and I felt the nub of the head on the outside of my right wrist. Nate had showed me how he'd escaped from zip ties in Iraq, and he'd showed me how easy it could actually be... if you knew what you were doing. When he'd taught me to do it, it was supposedly to make the story more authentic, though he swore it would come in handy if I was ever abducted. Either way, the principles were the same, and at the moment, who I was going to be escaping from was likely to be changing. The groan of metal came again, and I heard one of the soldiers call out.

"Stand down or I will open fire!" he barked. There was a snap of leather when Deacon pulled his arm free of the table. I tried to ignore his efforts and focused on getting the fastener of the zip tie worked around until it was in the middle of the gap between my wrists and away from my body. The rounded edge of the chair back made that harder, but I finally managed to work it most of the way there. Deacon laughed and I heard another snap, then the staccato explosion of gunfire in a large, bare room.

"Is he dead?" the other guard asked. I looked over to see Deacon laying back against the table with three closely spaced holes in the center of his chest. Black blood trickled from each one, but not enough to make me believe he'd been alive when he'd been shot.

"Fucker took three to the chest, man," his buddy said confidently. "He ain't gettin' up from that."

"They get up," I said. "Put one through his forehead to make sure."

"Shut the fuck up," the shooter said. "Call it in," he told his partner.

"Mr. Sikes is gonna be pissed," his partner said as he thumbed his mic. From outside, the sound of gunfire erupted, at first sporadic cracks from assault rifles, then longer bursts from the bigger guns punctuating the radio chatter between the guards and whoever they were talking to. When the slower *thump-thump-thump-thump!* of heavy machine guns started up, the two men looked at each other with the first signs of concern on their faces. I'd only heard one gun that sounded like that, the M2 or "Ma Deuce", a fifty caliber machine gun that had been in the US military armory since World War I. Even an Air Force Communications Signals Intelligence specialist picked up a basic knowledge of firearms, and a tour in Iraq made sure I got to see and hear them a lot closer than most people, even if I'd barely left the Green Zone in Baghdad. I could just imagine the amount of damage the heavy gun was doing, but some part of me knew it wasn't nearly enough. There were more than a hundred and fifty thousand people in Springfield, and no matter how many rounds the military had, I was guessing they didn't have more than a few hundred men and women crammed onto the containable areas of Missouri State University. And I was most likely in one of the larger defensible places, McDonald Arena. There was a tunnel that connected McDonald to the football stadium, which would make a decent landing field or staging area, if not an ideal one. With the heavy iron fence that circled the field, zombies and ghouls would have a hard time getting in if they had fortified the choke points, but it was far from impregnable if they all decided to rush it at the same time. The problem was that zombies didn't *think*. Even ghouls were outsmarted by door handles. What had made them all rush the fence now? I turned my head and looked over at Deacon. Instead of feeling happy that he was dead, I felt a pressure behind my eyes, like I needed to dismember him and burn the parts. Some deep instinct told me he was part of what was going on.

The sound of feet on the hardwood of the court's floor drew my attention away from Deacon. Four men in green scrubs followed a woman in a white lab coat. Two of them wheeled a gurney while the third and fourth carried bulky cases. The doctor looked at the two guards when she got to the door of the cage, and the shooter pulled a set of keys from his belt and unlocked it for her.

"Keep that door open, gentlemen. We won't be a moment," she ordered as the four men hustled inside. "I want tissue samples, blood and saliva as well as mucus. Get me a sample of brain tissue, too." she said. One of the orderlies carrying a case nodded, and they went to the body with cold efficiency. As they unstrapped Deacon's body, I felt my muscles tense slightly. If I was going to try to make an escape…and if I could survive a gaping chest wound…this would be the moment when I'd make my move. Something told me Deacon could.

"He's not dead," I said as they laid him out on the floor. One of the orderlies put his hand to Deacon's neck, then looked at me with a smile.

"He doesn't have a pulse. Seems pretty dead to me." He chuckled as another orderly laid out a body bag next to the corpse. "If he was gonna go zombie on us, he would have by now."

"He was already a zombie. No pulse doesn't mean-" I got out before Deacon's hand shot up and grabbed the orderly by the neck. The guy's scream ended in a wet gurgle as his throat was ripped out. The second orderly jumped back long enough to buy himself one more second of life before Deacon's teeth were on his neck as well. Blood sprayed across my cell as Deacon let his second victim fall to the floor with a gurgling sound. He ignored

106

the other two guys to grab the doctor by the throat and squeeze hard. An ugly, wet crunching sound filled the arena before he let her go and turned to face the remaining four men. She staggered back with her hands to her throat and her mouth gaping, trying to draw a breath that wouldn't come.

I clenched my teeth and turned away from the slaughter going on in the next cage. I had priorities of my own. Surviving was big on that list. It took an effort of will to ignore the screams as I stood up and pulled my arms over the top of the chair back, but I managed it. Once I was upright, I bent at the waist and pulled my arms back away from my butt as far as I could and clenched my fists, then brought my hands back down against my butt as I pulled my elbows out, away from each other. A line of fire wrapped itself around the outside of my wrists, but I brought my hands back again. This time, I remembered to turn my wrists at the same time as my hands hit my back and I tried to chicken-wing my arms. All of the force of the blow centered on the hasp of the zip-tie, the single weakest point on the whole device, and it popped free, releasing my arms. I turned back to the carnage in the cell next to mine.

One of the guards was crumpled against the bars of my cage, his head twisted around so that he was looking over his shoulders at me. The other was on his knees in front of Deacon, who had his hands on either side of the man's skull. With a barely visible effort, Deacon brought his hands together, and the man's skull deformed. I was never so glad to be looking at a man's back as I was just then. Deacon looked at me and gave a bloody smile, then he turned back to face the doctor, who was wide eyed and gurgling on her bottom, leaning up against the far wall of his cage. He walked to her with a deliberate care, his head tilted to one side as he squatted down to watch her choke to death. With his attention on her, I went to the first guard and pulled his body around so that his belt was closer to me and grabbed the keys from his belt, then grabbed his pistol from the shoulder holster under his left arm.

"You know how you can tell if they're dead?" Deacon asked as I looked the gun over. My head came up, but he was still watching the doctor. I palmed the keys and got to my feet.

"They stop moving?" I asked as I moved away from the bars.

"No. Shot a guy in the head once. He kept kicking for a few minutes, but that's the thing with a head shot. You know they're dead right like that. First thing he did was piss himself. See, her eyes are all glassy, but...ah, there it is. She's gone." He stood with a satisfied look on his face and walked over to the wall of iron bars that stood between us.

"So, now what?" I asked him. He reached down and pulled the dead guard's body away from the bars before he answered.

"Now I walk out of here like a free man and you die in a cage. Kinda fitting, don't you think?" He walked to the body of the other guard and started undressing him.

"Not really," I said. He ignored me as he pulled the guard's clothes on, then stood with his hat in one gray hand.

"You're going to listen to the people around you dying, and you're going to know that your turn will come soon. And I'm going to come back in here to watch you panic as my zombies surround your cage and tear it apart. I wonder...are you the kind of guy who thinks he can take on a thousand zombies with a single magazine and survive, or will you save the last bullet for yourself? For that one, last act of cowardice."

"I'm full of surprises," I said, and instantly damned my big mouth. He looked at me, and again, he tilted his head to one side, giving me a calculating look.

"You're right," he said and turned to walk toward the open door of his cell. He walked to the door of mine and a slow smile spread across his desiccated features. "I should just kill you now." He pulled a set of keys from his belt, sorted through them until he found the right one and inserted it into the lock. I bolted for the door, and he grabbed me by the hair. Instantly, I planted the barrel of my pistol in the crook of his elbow and pulled the trigger twice. The room seemed to explode as the report hammered my eardrums, but he pulled his mangled arm back. Dried lips peeled back from bloody teeth, and he backed up a step. All I could do was throw my shoulder into the door when he did the same from the other side. The door gave a few inches, but I pushed it shut. Undaunted, he stepped back again, his mouth moving. When he launched himself forward again, I stepped to the side, and he met no resistance when he hit the door. His momentum carried him halfway across the cell and he tripped over the chair I'd been sitting in. The door swung open behind him, hit the wall of the cage and rebounded back. I grabbed it, stepped outside, swung it the rest of the way closed and turned the key until the bolt clicked home, then pulled it half way out and snapped it off.

"Told you I was full of surprises," I said from a few steps away from the door. Even through the ringing in my ears, I heard his screams. It was my turn to go to a dead guard and get dressed. In my case, however, I grabbed his black t-shirt but left the blouse, and put the tactical vest on. I also picked up the man's assault rifle. It looked a lot like an M16, and the receiver group matched exactly, but it didn't have the carrying handle over the receiver. The telescoping buttstock looked different too, and it had Picatinny rails all the way around the barrel. It had the H&K brand on the left side of the magazine well, and I guessed it was one of the H&K Mk 416s Nate had spoken highly of. Once I was dressed, I had my choice of handguns. The guard Deacon had stripped carried a Colt Python on his hip, while the one I'd stripped had carried a SIG with the Blackwater logo on it. When I checked the magazines, I counted twenty rounds, which meant the SIG won hands down.

"I'm going to kill you!" Deacon screeched as I pulled the magazines for the rifle from the other man's tactical vest and stuffed them into my cargo pockets. My hearing was starting to return, but I wasn't going to be writing any music reviews for a few days. "I'll eat your heart, I'll rip your balls off and shove them down your throat!" The sounds of gunfire were now punctuated by the sounds of men screaming. I stood and put the earpiece from the vest's radio in my ear, then picked up the Python from the gurney.

"Do you hear me?" Deacon screamed.

"I hear you," I told him as I walked to the door. "I just don't care."

"I'm your new god, you stupid little fuck! This is my world now, and you're just a walking piece of meat! I am gonna rule the fucking world!" He stood at the bars and raved at me, and if he'd been alive, I imagined spit would have been frothing on his lips. I stopped at the corner of the cage and turned to face the abomination that had once been a man, then brought the revolver up and shot him through the kneecap. He howled in pain as he collapsed onto the floor, then started laughing again.

"You can't kill me with that," he said gleefully.

"Not trying to," I said flatly as I shifted my aim. I turned the other knee into paste and raised the barrel to his hips. The gun roared twice, and his pelvis was a bloody ruin. The fifth shot went through the ball socket of his left shoulder. "I figure you're going to live no matter what I do. I can't kill you, but I can damn sure fuck you up hard. But that…that isn't the worst thing. See, for all your power, you're no match for a good man with a little knowledge. You have to live … or whatever…with knowing that." I grabbed my cell phone and my sweatshirt off the table then turned and walked toward the door, one ear on the radio chatter, and less than half my attention on Deacon.

"I'll have the last laugh, mother fu-" he got out before I turned and put the last round in the Python round through his face.

"Not today."

Chapter 10

A Good Man...

It is the task of a good man to help those in misfortune

~ Sophocles ~

There were steam tunnels running under the southern half of the MSU campus. One came up near the locker rooms in McDonald Arena, in a utility room. When I'd worked campus security two years before, we used them during the winter to check various buildings or get around campus without being seen. Right now, they were my route to freedom and survival. Outside, I could hear gunfire as a near constant white noise. I turned the volume up on the radio as I headed down the hallway toward the locker rooms.

"No!" Keyes voice came over the radio. In the background, I could hear the sound of a helicopter's rotors. "They're not important, don't wait for them. We have Mr. Sikes on board, that's all that matters. Get this thing in the air!" I pulled the radio out of its pocket and thumbed the preselect to the next frequency, and all I got was the sound of grunting and chewing. So much for that position. The next one was pure static, but the next few were full of chatter.

"We're being overrun here!"

"...need more ammo! The fifty's run dry and we're down to sidearms!"

"Roger, Drifter, we are airborne now, heading to staging area one to extract the big dog."

"Negative, Ranger Six, staging area one is a no go, repeat, area one is no go!" I stopped in my tracks as Adams voice came over the line. Sporadic pops filtered in from the background. The heavy iron hatch was in front of me, literally under my feet. Escape was all but a given, all I had to do was keep going. Instead, I stopped the scan and listened.

"Karma One, can you make point bravo?" I heard the voice of Ranger Six ask. I pulled the hatch open and slid down into the

111

cramped concrete tunnel. All I had to do was go north, and I'd slip out beneath the feet of the zombie horde. The radio signal went staticy as I crouched there and listened.

"Negative, Ranger, negative. Command post is secure, but we have no exit. The stadium is overrun, and they're starting to swarm the field." Adams' voice was resigned, sounding like a man who knew he was not going to live much longer. I looked north, toward freedom, then south and recalled the last part of the Airman's Creed. *I will never leave an Airman behind, I will never falter and I will not fail.* I cursed, then thumbed the transmit button on the radio.

"Karma One, this is...uh, Tertiary. Do you read me?" I said into the mike.

"Who the hell is this?" Ranger Six demanded. "Clear this channel!" A few seconds passed, then Adams voice came back on the line.

"Tertiary, what is the status of Primary?" he asked.

"He's busy chewing on some lead. Karma, what is your position? Are you in the press box on top of the home team bleachers?"

"Affirmative Tertiary. Recommend you evac any way you can."

"Can't do that, Captain. Can you make it down into the lower levels? I can get you out." More silence, then his voice came over the radio again.

"Yeah, Tertiary. What is our rendezvous point?"

"When you see me, aim for where I am."

"Roger that. We'll be waiting." I didn't bother to sign off, I just pulled the trap door shut above me and took off south, heading deeper into the shit and cursing myself for an idiot all the way. I hustled as fast as I could in the pipe-lined tunnels, but it was still pretty slow going. In a couple of places, I had to duck under crossing pipes and conduits. By the time I came to the first turn I was dripping sweat. I passed the east facing tunnel and kept going straight until it ended in a T, then turned west, to my

112

right. By now, I was under the fifty yard line, probably right beneath the big maroon bear in the middle of the field. Another two hundred feet further on, I found myself at the little cutout that led up into the lower levels of Plaster Stadium. The tunnel led back north from here, angling toward Temple Hall, the science building.

I stopped there, and took a moment to get my game face on. From here, things were going to get hairy. As soon as I came up out of the tunnels, I was a target for any ghoul or zombie out there. For a moment, I felt myself balance at the edge of full blown panic as I got the full impact of what I was about to do. I wasn't a soldier, I was just a guy with a gun. Granted, it was a fancy gun, but that didn't make me special or invulnerable.

"Fear is what makes you smart," I told myself quietly. "Only a dead hero isn't afraid." I was just a guy, but I was a guy with a plan, and that put me two steps ahead of most people today. I slung the assault rifle and climbed the ladder up to the trap door, then shoved it up and open before I could think too much about what the hell I was about to do.

The trap door came up in another utility room filled with the usual assortment of pipes and supplies, among them a roll of the universal repair kit known as duct tape. The door unlocked from the inside, and a little duct tape over the latch kept it from catching behind me. It also conveniently marked the door for me for later. I pulled the door flush and made my way toward the stands, coming out of the concrete breezeway right on the fifty yard line. I could see a mix of zombies shuffling around and ghouls running back and forth across the limited field the breezeway offered. Once I could see the field, I unslung the bulky H&K and belly crawled until I could see sky. Above me, I could see the stadium lights glaring against the night sky. The sound of helicopter rotors and gunfire was now punctuated by near constant screams of dying men and the hungry moan of the zombies. I made my way to the low wall that separated the stands from the red surface of the running track that circled the field, then turned over so I could see the press box. There was vague movement behind the glass, so I keyed the mic on my radio.

"Karma One, this is Tertiary, do you copy?" I said softly.

"Roger, Tertiary," Adams voice came through, this time much clearer.

"Look down at the field. Do you see me?" I said, then waved my right hand.

"Roger that. We see you. We're ready at the door." I could hear the grin in his voice.

"When it goes dark, get yourself down to the field. I'll meet you there." With that, I turned around and crawled back into the lower level. One of the other duties we had when I worked security was letting the faculty into the stadium early in the mornings to turn off the lights just before daybreak. I'd only had to do it a few times in the six months that I'd worked there, but I remembered where the fuse boxes were. Less than a minute later, I was facing the panel, and wondering which ones did what. Without enough time to figure the whole thing out, I pulled the flashlight from my newly liberated tactical vest and turned the knob to the red LED light before switching it on. Then, I reached for the four large circuit breakers labeled "Main" and started flipping them to the off position. The lights went out inside and outside, and I found myself plunged into darkness for a few seconds until the emergency lights came on.

"Drifter, this is Ranger Six, we have Karma on thermal," I heard over the radio. "Hostiles moving their way. We have a shot, request clearance to engage."

"Ranger, you have a go to engage at will. I say again, engage, engage."

"Roger that, Drifter. Lighting zak up. Karma, keep your heads down. Engaging tangoes with door guns." I made it to the stands in time to see tracers arcing toward the stadium from the darkness in a steady stream. On the heels of the first rounds came the ripping sound of a minigun and the deceptive tapping of bullets hitting concrete and aluminum. Interspersed with that were the slapping sounds of lead making violent contact with flesh. Then there was only the distant sound of gunfire again.

"Hostiles down," Ranger Six said a few seconds later. I waited in the darkness with my light covered until I heard the soft shuffle of feet, then the thump of someone dropping onto the steps above me. Two more thumps came, then I heard the clanging of someone hitting the aluminum benches.

"Karma, we count six hostiles moving your way from the southeast," Ranger's voice came over the radio. I popped my head up and saw a group of figures running toward us across the field. Without the stadium lights, I was guessing that they were heading for the sound instead of anything they'd seen. It was enough, though. The assault rifle came up to my shoulder and I squeezed off a burst, knocking one of the dark figures down and staggering another. I adjusted my aim and fired a longer burst, and saw the flash image of a blond girl in a purple shirt and jeans take three rounds to the chest and the darker skinned guy with short dreadlocks in a button down shirt and slacks behind her drop. Another figure also dropped, but I didn't see any details. I felt a pang of guilt at shooting them, mostly because both looked like they weren't old enough to drink. It didn't stop me from emptying the magazine into the rest of the group and putting another two of them down. Fighting the urge to draw my pistol, I grabbed a new mag, hit the magazine release and slid the new one home. The urge to bring the gun back up and pull the trigger was strong as I heard feet slapping against the track, but I remembered to pull the charging handle back and release it before I did. When I brought the gun up, the muzzle flash showed me an older woman in a business suit jerking as I emptied half the new mag into her. Movement to my right caught my eye, and I saw a group of ghouls racing across the field. I tried to keep my burst short, but the gun clicked empty after three pulls of the trigger. The rational part of my brain knew I didn't have the trigger discipline to go full auto, and that I was going through ammo too quickly. Again, I changed the magazine as fast as I could, then took the extra second to switch the selector to three round bursts after I primed a round. The optical sight lined up on the lead ghoul, a huge guy silhouetted in the light of the buildings behind him, and I pulled the trigger. He tumbled and I moved to the next target, then the next, pulling the trigger only when I had a target. More gunfire came from above

115

and behind me and my target rich environment thinned a little more. I dropped a ghoul on the left of the advancing wave of undead, then the firing pin fell on an empty chamber.

"Reloading!" came a voice from behind me, and I repeated the call as I grabbed another magazine from the cargo pocket. Suddenly, two men came up and knelt down beside me, guns up and blazing. A hand fell on my shoulder, and Adams pulled me back toward the breezeway.

"Come on!" he yelled over the sound of gunfire. "Get us outta here!" I nodded and headed into the breezeway. Adams was beside me with his pistol up. He'd attached a suppressor to the bulky sidearm, and he reached up to flip up his NVGs once we got into the dimly lit interior.

"They're getting back up!" I heard someone behind us call out.

"Switch to semi-auto and go for the head shot!" another voice replied. There was a moment of silence, then I heard the single pops of semi-automatic fire. I clicked my light on again and kept my eyes to my right, looking for the shine of duct tape against the jamb. When I got to the long hallway that ran lengthwise under the stands, I uttered a curse. Somewhere in the dark, I'd taken the wrong turn, and I'd come out the wrong breezeway. A glance to my left revealed the red exit sign for the south doors, so I must have stopped short in the dark after I'd shut the power off. Turning to my right, I headed north. The sound of combat boots on concrete came from behind me, and I felt my shoulders twitch a little. Silence was as much a shield as darkness, but we also had to hurry.

Movement in the hallway ahead of us pulled me up short, and I pointed the light ahead of us. A woman in a dark colored shirt with Greek letters over her right breast turned to face us, and I could see something dark glistening on her face. Without a word, Adams brought his pistol up and pulled the trigger. The gun coughed in his hand, and the woman dropped with the left half of her skull missing.

"Turning right in the main breezeway. Zak is in the house," he said into his radio as we pressed forward.

"Falling back, Captain," someone replied. The gunfire was almost constant now, and I heard someone call out "Reloading!" behind us. Two more yelled it in quick succession, then I heard the sharper sound of pistol fire and curses. I picked up the pace, jogging along until I came to the next breezeway. I skidded to a stop and poked my head around the corner, then jumped back as teeth snapped together less than an inch from my nose. This time, I didn't scream like a little girl. I managed a more manly expletive as I jumped back, then Adams' right hand snaked over my shoulder and his gun barked again. Something wet sprayed my face and when I opened my eyes again, I could see more zombies shuffling toward us, backlit against the opening of the breezeway. The bulk of them were on the far side of the door we needed to get to, but the balance was shifting with every second on that. The captain took a step to my left and kept firing. His first two rounds dropped a zombie apiece before I could bring the H&K up. With the optical sights and the light from behind my targets, it was a lot easier to line up shots. I pulled the trigger and shifted my aim as one went down, then had to line up on the second one again when it didn't go down the first time. The third and fourth went down with one round to the head each, and the right side of the fifth one's skull disappeared on my second try. Beside me, Adams was firing methodically, sweeping from the left side of the hall, while I aimed for the center. Someone stepped up on my right and started unloading rounds from a suppressed pistol as I found my bullet count climbing through the mid-twenties. When I dropped the mag and called out that I was reloading, he put a hand on my shoulder.

"Wait for Adams to reload, son," he said, and I nodded to him. When I heard the next mag drop, I brought my rifle up and took aim. Three heads were in my scope, and I pulled the trigger three times, then the breezeway was clear for the moment. I went forward and checked the door on my left, breathing a sigh of relief when I saw the shine of duct tape next to the handle. Gunshots still rang out behind us, then I heard shouting. Adams and the man with him went back to the main hallway while I stayed at the door. More gunfire erupted, and men came barreling around the corner. Two stayed at the intersection and kept firing in both directions while Adams and the older man helped another soldier into the breezeway with another man them.

"Clear south!" someone called

"Contact north!" another voice said.

"Mason, see what you can do for Vasquez," Adams called out, but the man pushed him away and stripped his vest off.

"No, sir," Vasquez said. "It's no use. I'm bit. I'm already starting to turn, I can feel it." He reached down and unclipped the straps of his holster from his leg, then unbuckled it from his hip and handed it to the older man.

"I have your back," Adams said grimly as he slid a fresh magazine into the butt of his pistol. Vasquez shook his head and pulled a pair of grenades from the vest at his feet and stuck his index fingers through the pins, then looked over his shoulder. When he turned back, his face was twisted into a parody of a smile.

"I got this, sir. I'll keep 'em off your back, you get the colonel outta here." He turned and headed for the corridor, then turned and stood there, facing north, chest heaving as he waited.

"God go with you, son," the older man said softly.

"Go!" Vasquez yelled, then he pulled his hands apart, yanking the pins from the two grenades and running out of sight. The two men at the intersection ran toward us. I pushed the door open and stepped into the utility room. As Adams and his men crowded into the small room, I tore the tape off the door, and it closed with a satisfying click behind me. A heavy *whump!* went off outside a second later, and I closed my eyes, thinking of Vasquez's courage. If I got bit, I couldn't hope for a better example of how to go. It took some shoving and squeezing to make it to the trap door.

"It's going to get tight down there, and hot," I said as I lifted the metal hatch. "We're going to have to stay single file most of the way. Some of the pipes are really hot, too." Six pairs of eyes looked at me, none of them showing more than a hint of the grief I knew they were feeling. It was Adams who broke the silence.

"Okay, Stewart, you lead. I'm behind you, Colonel Schafer, you're behind me. Mason, Carter, then Jackson on the back end. Suppressed sidearms, people." Rifles were slung and the other Green Berets pulled bulky pistols similar to the one Adams had been using. "Stewart, shuck that Blackwater rig and put on some real gear." He handed me Vasquez's tactical vest with a look that brooked no argument. The Blackwater rig, as he'd called it, was lighter but I suspected it wasn't as well armored. The vest he'd handed me felt like it weighed three times what I was taking off. I grabbed the radio and did a quick check of the pockets for anything useful. Most of what I found was gear that I'd find in the military vest, but the left chest pocket yielded a wallet with some cash and ID. Once I'd shrugged into the camo vest and buckled it into place, he handed me the holster to strap to my leg.

""Draw it," he said once I finished buckling it to my leg. I pulled the pistol and held it up, barrel pointed at the ceiling. "H and K Mark twenty-three Mod zero. Mag release, slide lock, safety, all ambidextrous. Twelve forty-five caliber rounds in the mag, if you're smart, one more in the pipe. Suppressor and LAM, or Laser Aiming Module. Activates when you put your finger on the trigger. Suppressor screws on counter-clockwise, and she field strips like the old Colt M1911. You don't put your finger on that trigger unless I tell you to. This pistol shoots better than you do, so if you miss, it's your fault. You got that?"

"Yeah, I got it. It's heavy."

"Get stronger. Suppressor on, then lead the way." He turned away and I fumbled the clunky suppressor onto the threaded barrel, then slipped down into the hole. The rest of the team followed me, and even the colonel hit the ground with a bounce. I led them back the way I came, then past the McDonald Hall access hatch. Now we were into new territory. The safety lights mounted in the ceiling kept us from stumbling too badly, but they were few and far between, and not even the military flashlight could completely dispel the darkness, and the smell only reminded me I was under several feet of concrete and earth. I could just imagine the shuffle of feet above me as zombies wandered the MSU campus, searching for food, never knowing that a veritable buffet was walking right under their feet.

The walk seemed to take forever as we made our way through the dusty tunnel, past off shoots that I knew led to some of the dorms. Sweat started to trickle down my face in the oppressive heat. An eternity later, we came to a dead end. I reached out and tried the door, but the knob stayed firmly in place. I looked to Adams and hefted my pistol, but he shook his head.

"I had keys to all the doors when I worked here," I explained. He gestured to one of the men behind us, and one of them shuffled forward to kneel by the door. He pulled a slim case from his pocket and drew two tools out, then went to work on the lock. A few seconds later, he was pulling the torsion bar to the side and the door opened onto another utility room and cooler air. The steps heading up to ground level was as welcome a sight as I'd ever seen, and I made a beeline for them.

"Where are we?" Adams asked.

"Greenwood Laboratory School, just across the street from Hammons and Hutchens Halls."

"Where is that compared to the parking garage by the big performing arts hall with all the glass and the fountains out front?" the colonel said.

"About a block south and a couple of streets west of there. There's a church between here and there. Last couple of big churches I saw weren't pretty." The colonel's face fell and he nodded.

"I know, son. We had to deal with that ourselves. And you're right, it wasn't pretty." The rest of the team nodded at that and made some affirmative sounding noises, which made my respect for them go up a notch or ten. I'd only seen it from a distance. They'd probably seen it much closer.

"Well, if it's all the same to you guys," I said, "I'm heading my own way after we get outside. Nothing personal, but our last meeting didn't end well, and you know where to go from here so it's not like you need me." Six pairs of eyes suddenly shifted away from me, and someone cleared their throat. I was about to head for the door when the colonel stepped in front of me.

"Keyes ordered him to kill you and the girl with you," he said sternly. "So don't be too hard on Captain Adams or his men. He saved your life."

"And he just saved ours without knowing that, sir," Adams said. "I think he's more than earned the right to be as hard as he wants." Schafer scowled at Adams over that, then turned to me.

"I can't argue with that. If you want to go your own way, I have no issue with you doing that. But, you did save my life and the lives of my men. You're a damn fine shot and you're cool under pressure. The least I can do is offer you a place on one of the evac choppers." My heart skipped a beat at the offer. I couldn't even bring myself to feel guilty about being tempted. Besides, it was one thing to be tempted. It was another thing entirely to give in to it.

"Colonel, I'm all misty eyed with gratitude for the offer. I really am. There'll be tears later on, I promise. But I'd be breaking my last rule of survival if I took you up on that. Rule twenty two: Watch out for your family and your friends. So, thanks, but no. I've got people waiting for me. I can't let 'em down."

"I understand, son. A man has to keep his promises." He stuck out his right hand and I took it. His grip was like iron, but he didn't play the squeeze game most macho guys seemed to. "It's too bad you enlisted in the Air Force. You'd have made a damn good soldier."

"Thank you, sir. Let's get you out of here. I don't know about you, but I have places to be."

"Hoo-ah!" one of the Green Berets said softly.

Chapter 11

Homecoming

You never know what events are going to transpire to get you home.

~ Og Mandino ~

The back streets of Springfield were empty on my trip home. From the looks of things as I'd made my way east across National, something had drawn every zombie and ghoul in the area to Plaster Stadium. My bet was that the something was Mike Deacon. He'd done almost as much to help me get home as Adams and his team had before we split up at Greenwood. I had five extra magazines for my SOCOM riding in my assault vest and a handful of First Strike rations in the rucksack on my back. Most importantly, at least to me, I had two challenge coins in my pocket, both passed to me when I'd shaken hands with Adams and Colonel Schafer. Between the two of them, I'd probably be set for drinks for life if I ever set foot in a bar again.

For the first half hour, I could hear the sound of helicopters lifting off and the faint rumble of diesel engines, but as I walked down Lombard Street, those sounds became fewer and fewer. Gunshots peppered the night, and the smell of smoke was on the cool breeze that came out of the southwest. As I got within a hundred yards of Glenstone, the last large road I had to cross on the way home, I heard the sound of metal and glass hitting something hard, and the boom of a transformer going up. When I came up beside a store specializing in fur coats, I could see a long swath of darkness to the south of me. Cars were nose to tail heading north along this stretch, but the southbound lanes were mostly clear. There were still no zombies or ghouls in the area, at least that I could see or hear, so I crouch-walked across the empty lanes to the narrow gap between a Mazda and a Cadillac. There wasn't enough space to squeeze between them, so I jumped on the Mazda's hood and crossed it in two steps before I jumped across to the trunk of a sedan. Then I was jumping back down on the concrete and hustling between two squat stone buildings. My path took me through the dusty driveway of Glenstone Block and by the fire-gutted remains of the building that used to house the tile and stone store. From there, I crossed the railroad tracks and found myself in a storage yard.

Even though I was in decent shape, I had to stop and take a break for a few seconds. It was one thing to walk five miles, it was another to do it hauling thirty pounds of gear and ammo. It had been a good four years since I'd had to do that.

"At least it's cooler than Baghdad," I said softly after I took a pull from the straw of my camelback. Then it was time to move again. Without a vehicle, I could cut between houses and across lawns, which cut a lot of distance off my trip. Without a ton of zombies wandering around, I could move a lot faster as well. Ten minutes later, I was cutting across Barnes Street and heading down the driveway of someone's house, then climbing the back fence and heading out between two houses at the end of a cul-de-sac. I didn't bother to read the street sign as I crossed the street that T-ed into the cul-de-sac. It was what was beyond it that I was heading for. Once I hopped the short fence in the back of the next yard, I was off the streets, and into undeveloped brush. This was Carver Park, and it ran almost all the way to Oak Grove. No houses, no people, just pure landscape between me and the road for about a quarter of a mile.

Once I was out of sight of the road and street lamps, pitch darkness ruled the night, so I pulled out my flashlight and turned it on. The red light was just enough to see by and to avoid getting poked in the eye by any low hanging tree limbs as I kept heading due east. I finally broke out into an open field, which made the going much easier until I got to the far side. A little searching revealed the trail I'd found a year before that led out to a vacant lot on Oak Grove. From there, it was less than three blocks to my street, but unlike every other trip home, I wasn't going to be aiming for the front door.

Instead, I passed my street and took a small drive that ran between two other houses off of Oak Grove into another small park nestled in the center of the block. If you didn't know about it, you might miss it. The street lamps were still working here and the neighborhood still had lights on, which made navigating without the flashlight a lot easier. With a bittersweet feeling, I unlatched the back gate to our yard and slipped inside. Our shed was on my right, with the big oak tree that I'd built Amy's tree house in on my left. The house was dark and quiet, but I wasn't taking chances. As quietly as I could, I went around to the side of the house and peeked over the fence at the front yard. Karl's truck was backed up against the front door, and Porsche's was in the driveway with Cassie's Wrangler behind it. I didn't see any vehicles along the street that I didn't recognize. One of the neighbor's cars was halfway through his garage door, and I could see movement in the car itself. A bicycle was laying in the middle of the street, and I didn't want to look too closely at the asphalt under it, for fear that the dark spot under it would resolve itself into a blood stain and drag marks.

I hopped down from the fence and made my way to the back door, reclaiming the hidden key I'd hung on a nail on one of the fence posts. A big bowl of cat food and another filled with water were on the porch, a sure sign Maya hadn't been able to find Leo, our big orange tomcat. The back door opened quietly, and I pulled the SOCOM before I ducked in and moved to one side, ending up beside the refrigerator. For a moment, I just listened. It was quiet and it stayed that way for a count of one hundred, then two hundred. If anyone had been here, they were probably gone. Of course, right now, anyone who might have thought about causing us trouble had other problems trying to eat them. Still, I wasn't about to stick around and make myself an easy target. I stood up and checked the living room, then did a quick look-through of the rest of the house. The key rack by the front door was empty, and the pantry had been methodically stripped, including the five gallon buckets of staple foods and the empty water jugs. Most of the photos were gone from the top of the entertainment center, with the frames left empty. Finally, I took a look in the garage, and only saw one bike hanging from the hooks in the ceiling. Once I was confident no one was lurking, I went back to our bedroom with a lighter heart. Maya had followed the plan and bugged out like I figured she would as soon as Cassie and Porsche had shown up.

Aside from the obligatory bed and dresser, Maya's and my room held one other feature of note: bookshelves. Before we'd bought our e-readers, we had invested heavily in paperback books, and thus, bookshelves. Aside from the two large shelves in our room, there was another one in the spare bedroom. We had enough books to stack them two high and two deep in the shelves, which made for great camouflage. I went to the shelf on the right side of the room as I stepped in and knelt down. Behind the books on the far left side was our fireproof strongbox. I grabbed it and headed for the kitchen. The strongbox made an audible clunk as I set it on the counter, then I turned to the freezer. Maya had one of the keys on her keychain, and we had kept another hanging on the key rack by the front door. We also kept a spare hidden in the freezer, encased in an ice cube at the bottom of the tray for the ice-maker. A few whacks with the meat tenderizer freed it, and I unlocked the strongbox moments later. Inside was half of the stuff I'd stashed in it. Ten silver ounces, three hundred rounds of .22 long rifle ammo, fifty rounds of .45 ACP and a set of unmarked keys were left. Maya would have the same stuff on her, except for the keys. Now I had almost everything I needed to bug out. I really wanted a hot meal, a hot shower and a few hours of sleep, but like the old poem went, I literally had miles to go before I slept. Of the three, all I was likely to get right now was a lukewarm meal.

I stowed the stuff from the safe and left it on the kitchen table, then opened the refrigerator. The big pot of Maya's chili was still there, though much depleted since I'd been at it last. A handful of crushed up Fritos and some shredded cheese before it went into the microwave added texture and…well, cheese, which I'd never known to make a meal any worse. When the microwave beeped, I took the steaming bowl and sat down at the kitchen table to eat, probably for the last time. It was a bittersweet moment. I was finally home, my destination since sunset yesterday, and I was alone. Worse, I was going to have to bug out and say goodbye to the home Maya and I had made over the past two years. When I'd prepared for this moment, I had always imagined us doing that together, which somehow took a little bit of the sting out of it when I thought about it.

126

My maudlin ramblings came to an abrupt end when I heard the back door thump against the jamb. The SOCOM was in my hand as my head came up, and the door rattled again. Only one creature on Earth without opposable thumbs was that insistent, and the thought brought a smile to my face as I went to the back door and looked through the glass panes. Sure enough, Leo was sitting on the porch, looking up at me with a fierce feline scowl, as if to say "Let me in asshole." I opened the door and he sat there for a moment, as if suddenly undecided about whether or not it was open wide enough, or if he really wanted in. Then he jumped across the threshold and head-butted my shins. I closed the door behind him and reached down to scratch the top of his head, but he had other ideas. As soon as I bent over, he reared up on his hind legs and put his front paws on my thigh. Leo is a big cat, and when he leans against you, you know it. When he wants up, there were two stages. This was the first one, the gentle request, which was to say, he hadn't pulled his claws out and started climbing up my side. My face broke into a smile as I pulled him up and he immediately planted his furry forehead against my cheek. There was a deep rumble like a chainsaw idling, his version of purring, and he curled up into the crook of my elbow, his favorite sleeping spot since Maya had first rescued him as a kitten two and a half years ago. Back then, he'd barely filled the palm of my hand. Now he felt like fifty pounds of orange fur and attitude snuggled up against me.

"I'm glad to see you," I told him as I felt my chest tighten. Maya and I had both had a soft spot for animals, and I knew it had to have been rough for her to leave without being sure of Leo's fate. I swear, he must have gotten a stray hair in my eye, because I had a moment of blurred vision. A furry paw reached up and tapped the side of my face before he head butted me again. Usually that was a reminder that I'd stopped petting or scratching far too soon, but just then, I could have sworn he was as happy to see me as I was to see him.

"You ready to get the hell out of here, ya big furball?" I asked. He answered me with a sort of purring chirp, and didn't protest when I set him down. Maya and I had planned for bugging out together and separately, and at the moment, I couldn't have been happier for it. I knew she was as safe as was possible right now, and she knew I would catch up to her if I could. Leo followed me as I went out to the shed and grabbed the shovel, then trotted along beside me as I went back to the garden along the west fence. We had sectioned it off from the rest of the yard with heavy, untreated railroad ties. With a tired creaking of my knees, I knelt down beside the one on the south side of the garden and flipped it over. Then, I started to dig. About a foot down, the shovel hit what I was looking for with the thump of metal against plastic. I tossed the shovel aside and started scooping dirt out with my hands until I had uncovered a four foot long line of black plastic tarp. It parted easily under the combat knife in my vest, revealing a six inch wide gray plastic tube with a thick nylon strap laying along its length. A little tugging pulled the whole thing free from the dirt. Underneath it was a quarter section of pipe that I'd cut a one inch square into. I grabbed it and brought both pieces inside. The section of pipe fit neatly over the cap at one end, and with some effort, I unscrewed the end to reveal the contents of my bug out cache. Inside was my Ruger 10-22, my venerable Colt M1911A1, a sword and a set of knives, three home made MREs, a Lifestraw and my basic survival kit. I opened the survival pouch and checked that everything inside was still in good shape. The poncho and mylar survival blanket were intact, as was the black canvas Direct Action Response Kit I'd bought from Dark Angel Medical. The DARK Kit was a stripped down, bare essentials kit with a tourniquet, shears, and the basic bandages necessary for serious wounds. It also had hemostatic gauze, a specially treated bandage that promoted quick clotting. It wasn't what Maya called a 'boo-boo kit' that you used for minor cuts and bruises. This one was for the serious stuff: gun shots stab wounds and major lacerations. It was the one kit I never wanted to have to use, and the one I was the most grateful to have. A flick of the disposable lighter produced a good flame on the second try, and the survival matches looked good. When I pulled out the chemical hand warmers, the seals were still intact, and the Mag light worked once I put the batteries in it. Food, water, shelter and light were all covered. The next part was defense.

I had stored the Ruger and the .45 field stripped, with a .22 revolver stashed intact with them just in case. I had the two guns reassembled and ready to load in about ten minutes. The Ruger had six magazines, the pistol had four. The cache had been stored with 100 rounds for each inside it, and a multi-tool for good measure. Each magazine was loaded slowly, every round checked before it went in the mag. The Ruger 10-22 was a fine little rifle. Lightweight, reliable and infinitely customizable, it had become the mainstay of my small arsenal. I had added a quick release lever for the magazine and a four power scope to mine. My .45 had been my grandfather's, and it had been given to me in his will. I'd grown up shooting that gun, and it had yet to let me down. It hit like a Mack truck, and it was deadly accurate. Finally, I pulled out the blades.

When I had bought them from Zombie Tools a year ago, the last thing I had on my mind was actually fighting zombies with them. I'd grown up with the idea that there was no excuse not to have a sharp knife on you at all times. In Missouri, like most of the Midwest and South, it was just something a man always had on him, whether it was a pocket knife or a fixed blade. Thus, the ZT Tainto was a must. Fourteen inches and fifteen ounces of 5160 carbon steel, it had been the first blade I had bought from Zombie Tools, and it had been hard to put it away in the cache. The second blade, though, was the one I found my hands itching for since I'd realized I was in the middle of a zombie apocalypse. Called the Deuce, it was as close to indestructible as I had ever seen, just tip heavy enough to hit like a sledgehammer but not as clumsy, and light enough to swing all day if I needed to but heavy enough to cut through most things. Right then, it definitely lived up to the Zombie Tools slogan "A fist full of fuck yeah." The last blade was actually six blades, two sets of ZT Spikes, throwing knives that could also be turned into rope darts with a few feet of paracord. I had picked them up for hunting small game and as a deterrent. The Tainto went on my belt, and I stowed four of the six ZT Spikes in a pocket on the tactical vest. The other two went in the leather sheath I'd made for them. Finally, I slung the Deuce in its Kydex sheath across my back. The SOCOM stayed on my leg, and the Colt's holster went on the vest, under my right arm. The Ruger I just slung over my shoulder. Armed and moderately prepared, I went back into the bedroom and opened my closet door.

Inside was only one thing I needed. I'd put it off until last because it felt like I was saying goodbye to the house, but it was that time. I needed to be on my way. Maya was waiting for me. With a deep breath, I knelt down and grabbed my own combat boots, then headed for the kitchen table again. The boots I'd taken from the guards at MSU had almost fit, but they weren't mine. Even 'almost' didn't fit well enough to keep blisters from forming if you walked long enough. This pair was broken in and they fit right. As soon as I slipped them on, I felt the difference; my feet were still sore, but they weren't being rubbed raw along the heel or the outside of my foot. I did a quick check of the other things we stored in the hall closet, but my other Ruger was gone, and so was my main bug out bag. Maya had stuck to the plan.

Leo followed me out to the garage, and sat on his favorite spot as I took my Schwinn down. As he perched on the cardboard box by the door, he followed my movements with half-closed eyes. The bike was still in good shape, but the air pressure in the front tire was low. That was easily enough remedied with the hand pump before I went to the bike trailer that I'd stored vertically against the wall. That was still in great shape, so I lugged it through the house and into the back yard, then went back and did the same with the bike. Leo followed me when I brought the bike out, then stopped on the porch and waited while I grabbed the bucket with his food and his inside bowls, and loaded the cache tube and the rest of my gear on the trailer. Finally, I grabbed my bolt cutters and crowbar out of the shed along with the bungee cords. Once I had everything lashed down under bungee cords, Leo hopped down off the porch, trotted over to the trailer, hopped up on top of it, then proceeded to turn around twice and plop down in a puddle of orange fur. I laughed at him like I did every time he did that.

"This isn't just a trip to the grocery store, you know that, right?" I said as I pushed the bike across the yard. He raised his head long enough to regard me with cool disinterest, then returned to his lounging. With his tacit blessing, I pushed the bike out through the back gate before I latched it behind me, then got on the bike and started pedaling across the park and toward the road. Faint gray light was gracing the sky on my right as I coasted down Oak Grove, and for the first time in hours, I heard birds start to sing. Their chirping covered any sound I might have made as I pedaled up the slight incline near the intersection of Cherry Street. I turned east and followed Cherry, watching the sky light up ahead of me. As the side streets went by, I tried to grab quick looks, but I couldn't see any movement in the dim light, even at the slower speeds I was going. Once I got past Belcrest, I was in more open ground, but it was still quiet. A couple of hundred feet before I got to the railroad tracks that crossed Cherry, I stopped at a small turn off that led to a dirt road.

Up until then, I hadn't risked using the front light on my handlebars, but I decided I was safe enough to reassure myself. The headlamp came free of the clamp, and I flicked it on. Leo gave me a look of mild interest as I crouched at the edge of the red clay road and played the light over it. Sure enough, after a little looking, I found what I was looking for: bicycle tire tracks. Six people tracking down the same road was going to leave a trail even a lapsed country boy like me could read. I wasn't going to be telling anyone how fast they were going or how heavily they were laden, but I figured they'd been this way. Another ounce of worry felt like it was lifted off my shoulders as I went back to the bicycle and put the headlamp back in its clamp. Maya had been okay at least up to here. No one else knew our bug out route, and only she would have known that you could only take that particular route on a bike.

Up ahead, I could see the first cars backed up from the overpass, and a few that had tried to go off road to get to 65 Highway. Most had gotten stuck in the softer ground. On the right side of the road, the remains of a Jeep smoldered in the dawn's first rays as the sun started to clear the trees in front of me. I looked to the path that Maya had led the others down, and I wanted to follow it. But I still had a stop to make. With the traffic backed up, I didn't want to risk running into any ghouls trapped in a car. For that matter, I had no idea if there were any survivors lurking around…or, more accurately, if there were any scavengers. I turned left, away from Maya's trail, and headed down Cavalier, the street directly across the road from me. Cavalier ran almost due north through an industrial park. Businesses went by on either side as I pedaled, places with their closed signs now permanent. A body shop, a gymnastics center, a shipping company…all silent now. The road curved left in front of an advertising company, but I kept going, letting the bike coast into their parking lot and turning right. The east end of the lot ended in a gravel drive about ten feet from a double gate. Black smoke rose in a thick column ahead of me, one of many that I could see now that the sun was up. I'd hoped it was further north, but from the looks of things, I was pretty sure it was coming from the same place I was going. My heart sank as I got off the bike and went to the trailer.

"Alright, you. Stay here," I told Leo. He looked at me reproachfully and laid his head back down. He knew the drill. Once I was on the bike, he stayed put until I started unloading the trailer or took him off of it. The first few trips out to our bug out retreat had been in a carrier, then he'd been allowed to ride in the open. All it had taken was one incident of him running off for him to figure out to stay with the bike until we unloaded. I went to the gate and cut the lock, then slipped through. The back fence was a joke, mostly there to act as a property line. I clipped the connecting points at the corner of the fence and pushed the chain link section away to create my own opening. From there it was only thirty yards to cross the railroad track and approach the rear of the storage facility where I'd stashed the rest of my bug out gear. A few more judicious clips with the bolt cutters and I was pulling the chain link fencing away from the southwest corner of the lot. Carefully, I made my way in, crouching in the ten foot space between the end of one row of storage units and the fence.

The bolt cutters had done their job, so I stuck the handle through my belt before I unholstered the SOCOM and screwed the suppressor on. I could hear the sound of flames crackling toward the front of the lot, and the low rumble of a diesel engine. For a moment, I stood there and listened further, and caught a few brief snatches of conversation, but nothing I could make out clearly. Someone was here, but how many someones? And where the hell were they?

The sound of a storage door being rolled up answered the last question. It sounded like they were midway down one of the rows. My small storage unit was near the end closest to me, less than ten yards from where I stood. I took a few slow steps forward and peeked around the corner of the building. The row was clear, and I could see my storage unit just a few feet away. As tempting as it was to sprint to it and grab my stuff, I couldn't do that. Each row was over a hundred yards long, and that was a lot of area with zero cover. If someone caught me coming out of my unit, I was in the deep end of screwed. So, I needed to catch the other guy out in the open. At least that way, I could decide if I could leave them alone or if the Texas defense of "he needed shooting" was justified. I double checked the safety, swallowed the tang of adrenaline in my throat and did a fast trot across the open section until I was behind the next row. A peek around the corner showed no one in sight, but I could hear people talking more clearly now. Another quick dash, and I was behind the third row.

This time, when I put my head around the corner, the row wasn't empty. A bright red truck on oversized tires was backed into the row. Several of the units were open, and I could see two men watching the front of the lot. A man in mismatched hunting camo emerged from the left side carrying a cardboard box. Another emerged from the other side with what looked like a gun case. The second one wore brown coveralls and a baseball cap, with a revolver holstered on his hip.

"Whatcha got?" the camo'd man asked.

"Benelli twelve gauge," the other one answered. "You?"

"Got some stuff for them girls we rescued. I think whoever had this place was a stripper or somethin'," he said as he set the box down on the tailgate and pulled out something black and shiny.

"Shit, Mike! We're not at the goddamned mall! Just look for stuff we can trade or use."

"We can trade the girls. Dress 'em up nice, maybe we can get more for 'em. Besides, they'd look better in this stuff." The man in brown seemed to think that over for a second.

"All right. Put it on the truck, but that's all. Start looking for stuff we can *use!*" My eyes narrowed as I watched them go back into the storage units. I wondered if "rescued" meant "kidnapped" or if the girls even knew what these men had in mind for them. Either way, it wasn't enough to start shooting. As I mulled the moral ambiguity in my head, I darted across the open space to the next row. Whether I ended up confronting these guys or not, I still needed to finish checking the area out before I did anything and I could still hear other voices from the other row. Rule seven applied here: Know your terrain. I holstered the SOCOM and unslung the assault rifle. At the ranges I was looking at, the pistol was useless.

When I took a glance around the corner of the third building, I was reminded of my twelfth rule of survival: Assume people suck after shit hits the fan, and that they're after your stuff. Somehow, this group had managed to hijack a prisoner transport vehicle from the sheriff's department, complete with two sheriff's deputies, one male and one female. The female deputy was handcuffed to the back of the transport, and the other deputy was in the middle of four other guys. Three of the scumbags had baseball bats, and the fourth one had a wicked looking bowie knife. They had backed the transport in at an angle to block off the front gate, and also hide most of the drive between the storage units from view of the street that ran in front of the place. Beyond the front gate, the manager's apartment was ablaze. Risking exposure, I brought the assault rifle up and peered through the four power optic and trained it on the deputy's chest. Over his left breast pocket, I could see the badge was a cloth patch sewn on to his duty blouse. The woman's badge was missing, which meant hers had to have been a metal one. Cloth badges were distinctive to corrections officers, while metal ones were given to patrol deputies. That told me which division they each worked for, and made my job a little easier. The four guys taunting the CO had made a mistake in letting him have his hands free. Corrections officers had to deal with physical confrontations with multiple inmates on a regular basis. This guy was in his element. His attackers weren't. Since he'd kept his blouse on, I was betting on him still having his vest on, which in a jail environment, was designed to protect him more against getting stabbed than shot. The guy with the knife was the least of his worries.

The moral ambiguity of the situation was gone as I drew back from the corner and made my way back to the other side of the building. Shooting was likely to draw ghouls and zombies, but I didn't really see any other choice. I waited until the two looters were back at the truck's tailgate to bring the rifle up and fire at the guy standing guard on the opposite side of the row from me. As he dropped I corrected my aim and fired at the guy in brown, then moved my aim point toward his buddy as he darted for cover. I pulled the trigger as the other guard came into my site picture, then fired again as I got close to my original target again. Four rounds downrange, and two bad guys down. I heard cursing and yelling from the next row over as I brought my aim point back to the guard on the near side and pulled the trigger. *Five,* I counted to myself as he dropped. The guy in brown was crawling toward the truck's right rear tire, so I sent a round at him, then ducked back behind the building. No gunfire came my way, so I popped back around the corner to see the camo'd guy scrambling for his buddy's pistol. I stroked the trigger twice and sent him sprawling, then ducked back and headed for the other side of the building. The CO had one of the bat carriers in an arm bar and was using him as a shield against the only other guy left standing. One of the other bat carriers was laying on the ground with his hands stuck between his legs and the knife wielder had his own blade sticking out of his belly. The rifle went back on my back and I drew the SOCOM again as I came out from the side of the building. I advanced at a walk while the CO spun his human shield around.

"Drop the bat!" I called out as I got closer. The guy turned his head to face me, and the CO shoved his buddy into him. They went down in a tangle of limbs, and before they could get to their feet, the CO had clubbed both of them back down. He turned to face me with a grim look on his face.

"If you're going to shoot me, then pull the trigger now," he growled. I lowered the gun.

"If I was going to shoot you, I would've done it from back there. Go ahead and unlock your friend. I'm going to go check the other guys. I'll be right back." I trotted over to the other truck and knelt by the guy on the driver's side. He had a pump shotgun with an extended tube and a sling, most likely a Remington 870 he'd taken from the deputies, and a Glock in a holster on his right hip. The other guy had an M-4, and the guy in brown wore a chromed revolver. I undid the gunbelts and took a look in the back of the truck. Tents, sleeping bags and camping gear shared space with a pair of plastic storage boxes and three gun cases. I popped the top on the storage boxes to find boxes of ammo in the first and coins in the second, smaller box. The gun cases held a pair of hunting rifles and a double barreled shotgun. Enough to help a pair of sheriff's deputies and a few other people stay alive a little longer. I grabbed the four guns I'd taken from the dead guys and headed back to two deputies. The one had uncuffed his partner and they were checking on the four women in the back of the transport. They had the one that the woman had nut-kicked cuffed and on his face on the ground.

"Got ya somethin'," I said as I held the long arms and the gunbelts out. The guy looked at me like I was trying to hand him a bag of snakes, but he took them.

"Why are you helping us?" he asked. "Not that I'm not grateful. It's just that almost everyone else we've met since this has all started has been trying to kill us."

"I'm one of the good guys," I said with a wry smile and stuck out my now empty right hand. "My name is Dave Stewart."

"Grant Jacobs," the deputy said, then pointed with his thumb over his shoulder. "That's Ann Tucker. We were out trying to rescue survivors when this group caught us by surprise. You're welcome to come back with us. The jail is the only safe place in town right now. We've got it barricaded and we have enough supplies to last for a while. We could use all the help we can get." Ann offered me a brief smile before she came over and squatted in the doorway. Grant handed her the Glock and pulled the magazine from the M-4.

"Thanks, but I've got a plan of my own. You're probably going to want to get out of town yourself. Look, there's a lot of gear, ammo and some more guns in the truck over there. Take it and get the hell out of here. Be careful when you head toward campus. Most of the dead were heading that way." I paused for a moment, unsure of how much more I should say. I had seen things in the past twelve hours or so that I was having a hard time believing even after seeing it.

"Thanks," Ann said as she buckled the sidearm on. "If the dead are heading toward SMU, the route back to the jail should be pretty clear. We should swing north a little to make sure we miss the shambling hordes." Grant nodded and slid the mag home and pulled the charging handle.

"Okay, you're gonna have a hard time believing this, but the zombies…a guy named Mike Deacon is controlling them." They both looked at me with open disbelief.

"You're kidding me," Ann said.

"I wish I was, but he pulled every zombie for at least three miles around toward the campus. As far as I know Deacon's still trapped in McDonald Arena."

"Mike Deacon? About five nine, dark hair, skinny little fuck?" Jacobs asked. I nodded and he laughed. "I knew that guy. He was a frequent flyer at the jail."

"Simmons brought him in on a domestic Friday night. I thought he died in his cell or something," Ann said.

"Yeah, he did," Grant said. "Guess it didn't stick."

"Well, I fucked him up pretty hard before I left the university," I told them. "Still, staying in town is probably a bad idea in the long run. Your best bet is to find a railroad track and follow it out of the city, then head northwest."

"Why northwest?" Ann asked.

"Population density's lower that way. Fewer people mean fewer zombies," I ad libbed. Nate's original wording had been that fewer people meant less competition for resources and fewer potential carriers if things went biological. Now I was seeing what he'd really been pointing me toward. I pulled a notepad and pen out of the pocket of my vest and scribbled down a frequency and times. "If you get up Wyoming way, tune in to this frequency. Or channel twenty six on citizen's band. Take care and good luck." I turned and started away.

"Hey, Dave," Grant called after me. I turned back to him. "Thanks again. If we ever get out to Wyoming, we'll look you up. Safe travels, man." I gave him a nod and headed back toward the truck. The stash of coins had been too good a find to pass up, so I stopped at the tailgate and pulled the smaller storage box toward me. Most of the coins were old nickels and dimes, but I hit paydirt in a small leather pouch: ten gold Krugerrands. I pulled five out and dumped them back into the box before I tucked the pouch into my vest. A small fortune in gold coins riding in my pocket was enough to put a spring in my step as I headed back for my storage unit. What I had there was worth more than all the gold on the planet just then. The storage unit door opened on my second bug out cache. Inside was my back up bug out bag, an Army ammo case and a binder filled with maps.

The bug out bag had a lot of the stuff I was already carrying, but it also carried more long term survival gear, including a small tent, a ground pad and a wool blanket. I tucked the maps into the tan pack then slung it across my back, grabbed the ammo case and slipped out the door. The sound of a truck pulling away reached my ears as I slipped out the back of the facility the same way I came in, then trucked across the tracks and headed for my bike.

Leo gave me a disapproving look as I stuck the ammo case in among everything else, but he stayed put otherwise. My bug out bag went on top, and he perched atop it like a little king on a padded throne. The bike took more effort to get going, but it was a light enough burden once I got moving. I followed my route back to the dirt road and turned down it. The brown clay rolled past below me, and the road turned to the south as it paralleled the tracks, the curved back to the east. I followed it under Schoolcraft Freeway to the area where the road construction crews that were widening the overpass parked their construction vehicles. A temporary crossing had been set up under the overpass, and I took advantage of it to get my bike on the north side of the tracks. Then came the ride up the hill. In a car, it would have been a pretty gentle grade, but on a bicycle, pulling more than fifty pounds of gear and a miniature lion behind me, it was torture. It finally leveled off and turned to the right, which put me on an access road called Eastgate that ran beside the freeway. Once I was on the street, I kept going north, and I breathed a sigh of relief. I was past the worst of the roads blocking my way out of the city, and even if I could see ghouls pawing at the glass of car windows, I was still away from the worst of the zombie clusterfuck that Springfield had become.

On my right, an empty road beckoned, and I took the turn, heading east again on a quiet residential road. The asphalt strip I was coasting down barely qualified as two lanes, but it was a straight as a nun's ruler and level. Now that I was free of the city, I could indulge myself a little, and put some miles under my wheels. I set my phone on the pad attached to my front handlebars and activated the app that controlled the electric motor mounted to my bike's rear tire. It hummed to life and I let my feet stop pedaling as it kicked in. Not much more than a disc inside my rear tire, the FlyKly motor would take me about twenty miles before its battery gave out. Even better, it would recharge as I pedaled or when I coasted downhill if I couldn't plug it in. I set the speed on the app to fifteen miles an hour and let the motor do its magic.

Once I turned north, I looked back to make sure Leo was still safe on board. He had propped himself upright on my bug out bag and was letting the wind ruffle his fur, his eyes slitted closed so that he looked more than a little smug as he rode along. We passed the Rolling Hills Country Club Golf Course, and I noted the irony that I was back on Cherry. The gentle hills and manicured landscapes on either side of me made it hard to believe that the world had pretty much come to an end not ten miles behind me, until I came across a man in pajamas wandering in the middle of a wide expanse of well kept lawn. Only a black iron fence stood between us, but as soon as he saw me, he sprinted in my direction. As he ran my way, I could see the blood staining his face, hands and the sleeves and front of his pajamas. He hit the iron fence at a dead sprint and bounced back with a meaty sound that left the fence vibrating and left chunks of him attached to the chest high points of the fence's top. As if only then recognizing that the fence was a barrier, he ran along beside it for a good five hundred yards without slowing down. When the fence curved away from the road, he stopped and watched me roll past, defeated by his inability to grasp that there was an opening less than a hundred yards away because it wasn't in his line of sight. As I passed him, I looked back over my shoulder to make sure he didn't get a sudden burst of common sense. He just stood there, straining against the fence, and I felt the urge to stop and put a pullet between his eyes grip me for a moment. From the corner of my eye, I could see Leo crouched down, his ears laid back and his teeth bared in a hiss, looking like I felt just then. One thing certainly stood out in my mind as I turned my attention back to the road in front of me: the ghoul had kept up with me all the way. He hadn't even slowed down.

Another thought struck me as I turned north again a few hundred yards later. The ghoul who had chased me had probably been in bed when he'd become infected. Had another infected bitten him, or had he come in contact with an infected? How far from a city did I have to go to find pockets of unaffected people? Or was pretty much everyone going to turn into zombies? Was I going to turn into one? Was Maya? Or Amy? Thoughts of them as ghouls and worse, as zombies, promised to give me nightmares as I cruised along the little farm road. The houses out here were set too far back from the road to see, and the prices were too high to purchase without an annual income that was at best stratospheric. I knew from personal experience. I'd tried to buy land in this area when I was setting up Sherwood, and my realtor laughed at me, then suggested I aim at something north of 44. So, here I was, aiming for a destination north of Highway 44. The road started to slope downward and I felt the slight resistance as the SmartWheel started to charge itself as I coasted into the cool, dark shadows of a tree covered stretch of roadway. It curved left, then bottomed out and angled back right as I crossed a creek and emerged from the trees on to another straight section. More green pasture and sporadic trees dispelled the apocalyptic nightmare I'd just survived, and I felt like I was just on another practice run out to Sherwood. I tried to imagine spending the weekend out in the woods with Maya, drinking beer and wine by the campfire. The last time we'd been out to Sherwood in August, we'd laid out on the grass and watched the stars overhead, and made love under the full moon.

Unbidden, the image of Maya suddenly turning ghoul and trying to rip my throat out inserted itself into my daydream, and I shook my head in revulsion. It was too early to start getting zombie related PTSD. Half a mile later, I started to doubt that, as I passed a little subdivision. Zombies wandered aimlessly down the side street, all of them moaning incessantly. I heard Leo growl behind me as we went quietly by, and I silently agreed with him. Minutes later, we passed the Rolling Hills High School (Home of the Fighting Spartans!), and I found myself hoping that the ring of unmoving bodies lying near the entrance to the school was the work of someone evacuating a bunch of kids last night. Then we were past, and none of the dead rose to follow me or try to eat me. I offered a silent prayer of thanks for small favors and pressed on, knowing the next two miles were the last easy part for a while.

The next half hour was quiet as I rode along, following the route Maya and I had spent three weekends perfecting, both in our cars and on our bikes, until I finally came to the last choke point. Maya had probably led everyone through here while it was still dark, which would have made things a lot easier for them. But as I pulled up to the overpass that covered 44, I found things a lot less convenient. In the daylight, I could see at least a dozen infected wandering around among the solid line of cars that blocked the road over the highway. There were narrow gaps between cars, but the dead filled a lot of them. A long, empty, open length of asphalt stretched between me and the overpass, so sneaking up on them in broad daylight wasn't an option, either. In fact, as I braked the bike to a stop, one of the dead turned my way and started shuffling in my direction. Others turned as it moved and followed it. A low, dreadful moan rose as more and more of them began to make their way toward me. A dozen became twenty, and I saw another group start my way from across the overpass, doubling their numbers. With the subdivision full of them behind me and this group in front of me, and God alone knew how many were on the highway, my options narrowed themselves down to only one: shoot my way through.

My first rule of survival was that staying alive is ninety-eight percent mental. Up to now, I'd been able to play things pretty smart, but I was pretty sure I'd finally been forced to make a dumb decision. I hopped off the bike and grabbed the Ruger plus a spare magazine from my vest. For what I was about to do, I needed its light weight and higher powered scope more than I needed the HK's higher powered rounds. The Ruger also had an almost non-existent recoil, which made it very easy to keep it on target, and it had the advantage of being the more familiar gun. I'd spent hundreds of hours practicing with it, and I'd put thousands of rounds downrange at Sherwood, aiming at cans and six inch targets. If there was one gun I knew I could pull off fifty consecutive headshots with, it was the Ruger, and with forty grain Velocitor rounds, I wasn't likely to need more than one shot for most of them. The sight picture came up and I brought the crosshairs down on a zombie forehead, then stroked the trigger. My trusty little 10/22 barked, and zombie number one dropped. The recoil was minimal, another reason I loved the .22 long rifle round, and I was able to put my sights on another zombie head in a heartbeat. Two shots, two really most sincerely dead undead. I took aim at another one, and it dropped, then moved from target to target until the first magazine was empty.

When the hammer fell on an empty chamber, I brought my right hand back and flicked the extended magazine release with my left middle finger. The empty mag dropped into the palm of my right hand and I popped the full mag in, then pushed the bolt back with my thumb to put the first round in the chamber. The closest one was still ninety yards away. Fifteen seconds later, I had nine more really dead zombies and two empty mags in hand,

and the shambling horde had almost covered another ten yards. I dumped the empties in a pocket and pulled another one out, popped it in and cycled the bolt back again with my thumb. Almost half the zombies were down, but they were getting closer, and my targets were getting bigger and easier to hit. Again, I emptied the mag, trying to keep my breathing even in spite of the rising sense of panic as they just kept getting closer, now less than sixty yards away. As I popped the fourth mag in, I looked over my shoulder to make sure nothing was creeping up behind me. The coast was clear, but the movement had let them gain another five yards before I put the lead shambler down. When the hammer clicked the fourth time, only a dozen or so were left standing about thirty yards away from me. As close as they were, they were also spread out further, and it took longer to get the scope on them. When the eighth one fell, the last five were twenty yards away, and I was almost out of time. The SOCOM would have given me more rounds, but it was in the holster on my right leg, and I didn't want to just drop the Ruger. I slung it across my shoulders as fast as I could right handed and pulled my Colt from its holster, then dropped into a Weaver stance and walked my fire from right to left, the forty five caliber skull-busters making paste of zombie brains from about ten yards away. Even that close, I managed to miss twice, leaving me with only one round in the mag when the last one fell.

Brass hit the ground with an almost musical *ping* as the echo from the Colt's last shot faded. When I lowered the pistol, I was treated to the sight of a hundred yards of bodies in front of me.

"Final score in the tenth round, Dave Stewart, forty five, zombies, zero," I said with a little more bravado than I had a right to. My shoulders were knotted and I took a deep breath for the first time in…I checked my watch…two minutes? It felt like I'd been shooting for an hour. The air smelled of cordite and something foul. I looked over my shoulder and saw that I'd finally gotten the attention of the urban zombie dwellers. Most were stumbling down the road, but a couple of ghouls emerged from the pack and broke into a run. I let out a tired sigh and grabbed the HK, then brought the ACOG's red dot down on the chest of the one on the right. Three rounds went down range, and his feet went flying out from beneath him. He landed on his shoulders, with his feet hitting the ground on either side of his head. I swung the sight over to the second ghoul and fired three more times. That one went stumbling and left a long smear of red on the asphalt before he slid to a stop.

"These fuckers just don't stop coming, do they, Leo?" I said as I unslung the Ruger and slid it under the bungee cords, then changed out the magazine in the HK and the Colt. Leo just looked at me with feline disdain and tilted his furry head. "Yeah, yeah, we're going." I hopped on the bike and started pedaling, weaving my way through the bodies. The bike fit between the front of a little Honda and a Ford F150, then I was on the overpass. It was surprisingly clear of vehicles, but 44 was clogged. Ghouls and zombies moved between the permanent traffic jam, some of them heading for the south side of the overpass. By now, I figured there was no one left alive down there. I kept my head low and prayed none of them looked up. Someone must have been watching over me, because I made it across without any new friends in my six. The road behind me was starting to fill with infected, but the way in front of me was mostly clear, and I could see nothing but open fields for nearly a mile in either direction. The gentle downhill slope went on for another quarter mile, and I let the Smartwheel recharge while I coasted. I was on the road, and on my way to Sherwood. The worst part, I hoped, was going to be how long it took to get there.

Chapter 12

Respite, Reunion & Revelation

Every parting gives a foretaste of Death, every
reunion a hint of the Resurrection.

~ Arthur Shopenhauer ~

Even after the world ended, Missouri was beautiful country. My route kept me on farm roads most of the way, with beautiful views to my left and right, green fields with trees just showing the first hint of autumn color in little groves that gave way to thick trees and gently rolling hills as I got closer to 65. The highway was nothing more to me than two bridges that I rolled under. Then I was back out in rolling fields and open road. Eventually, I saw the sign I was looking for, announcing that I was a mile from Fellows Lake. Wooded lots crowded up on the left side of the road, and thicker copses of trees started cropping up on my right. The road sloped down again, and I found myself coasting through a series of gentle S curves, then I was cruising across the bridge over the northern arm of the lake. To my right, it looked like it was a huge pond, with a thick covering of green moss on the surface a hundred yards out. On my left, the lake was blue and vibrant. A few boats were out on the water, and I got the impression that they were probably some of the few safe people in the area. In October, there weren't many people out on the lake and most of the casual boaters congregated on the southern arm anyway. The only other sign I saw of people was a blood trail leading off the road on the north side of the bridge. I followed the twists and turns that took me off the lake's shore and deeper into less cultivated areas, and in another half hour, I found myself slowing down to take the last turn before I got to Sherwood. Asphalt gave way to parallel ruts of packed dirt and rock, and I switched the motor off to cover the last half mile on my own. The road curved to the right and then snaked back left before I hit the last hundred yards, which ran pretty much straight.

I heard a deep booming bark start up when I got about fifty yards away from the hand-painted sign that marked the entrance to Sherwood, and a few seconds later, Sherman bounded out to the road. I coasted to a stop by the sign and stuck my hand down for him to sniff.

"Good dog," I said as he gave me his slobbery seal of approval. From behind me, I heard a warning growl from Leo. Sherman immediately bounced to the back of the bike to look the new arrival over. A hundred pounds of black and brown Rottweiler faced down fifty pounds of orange tomcat for a few seconds. Leo reared back and raised one paw in the air in warning. Sherman stuck his nose forward, and Leo's front paw turned into a blur. I expected it to turn into a free for all as I tried to get off the bike in time to save my cat from my new-found canine friend.

As fights went, it ended quickly. Sherman's head snapped back and his brow sort of wrinkled as he tilted it to one side. Then, he dropped down on his forelegs and rolled over to show his belly. I stopped in mid-stride, and Leo, apparently satisfied with the newcomer's show of fealty, hopped off the trailer. With his usual feline nonchalance, he strutted over to Sherman, swatted his nose again for good measure, then hopped back on the bike trailer to reclaim his mobile throne.

The sound of footsteps behind me brought me around, and I found myself being rushed by Maya and Amy. "Don't you ever do that to me again," Maya said into my shoulder while Amy got her arms around her mother and me from the right. My ribs creaked in protest but I was giving as good as I got, my fears laid to rest for the moment. Over her shoulder, I could see the others come out onto the road, every one of them armed, even Bryce. Porsche had the M-4 I'd been carrying, Bryce was carrying his Ruger and Karl was toting his Mini-14, while Cassie's pistol was holstered at her hip. Porsche's work clothes had been replaced with a pair of Maya's jeans and one of her t-shirts, but everyone else was still wearing what I'd last seen them in.

"No promises," I said softly. "But I'm pretty sure I don't have to worry about being captured by the Army again." She pulled away and gave a weak laugh, then reached up to touch my face for a moment.

"I thought I'd..." she started.

"Me, too. But you didn't. I'm okay, baby. Not even the zombie apocalypse can keep me away from you." I kissed her hard, and when we came up for air, we were surrounded by the rest of the group.

"How did you get away?" Porsche asked.

"Did you kill a lot of zombies?"

"Were you followed?"

"What's next?"

I held up my hands and shushed them. "I just got here guys. Let me at least sit down for a minute first!" I said. Amy took control of my bike and started pushing it while I fell in behind her and finished my trek to Sherwood. I reached out and touched the hand-painted wood sign Maya had made as we passed it, and took a quick glance around as we headed for the picnic table and the fire pit that were the center-piece of our little clearing. Our little shelter house looked okay, and the two storage buildings seemed undisturbed. A little further back, I could see the old windmill and the stone and wood barn that had been all that was left of the original farm, its blades turning steadily in the morning wind. Beside it were two blue metal cargo containers that were padlocked shut. Another degree of tension eased from the knot in my shoulders, and I sat down at the wooden picnic table feeling a little better. Maya put a brown bottle in front of me with a bottle opener beside it as she sat down beside me. I popped the cap on mine, and we touched the necks of our opened bottles together before we took the first swig from them. The first taste of Gwydion's Heartland Ale was like nectar of the gods on my tongue, and I fought down a pang of grief at the thought of how many people I knew who might be walking around dead right now. Gwydion made a damn good ale, and Maya had traded him several pieces of period garb for a case of his home-brewed liquid gold.

"Come on, Dave," Bryce said eagerly. "How'd you get away? Who were those guys, anyway?"

147

"Okay," I said, bowing to the inevitable. "Here's what happened." I laid out the highlights of what had happened after I was captured, leaving out the more gruesome details and leaving off after the shoot-out at Highway 44. "Now it's your turn. How did your trip go?"

"Slowly," Porsche said.

"As soon as they showed up, I got everyone packed up and out the back gate," Maya picked up the story. "That took us almost an hour, then the trip here..." she paused and shuddered. "It was dark, and we had to take it slow most of the way. My bike was the only one with a motor, so we pedaled it the whole way. We heard people screaming even after we got out of town. We finally had to stop after we got to Fellows Lake. There was some trouble there." She stopped, and Karl put his hand on her shoulder.

"She had to shoot a man," he said quietly. "He pulled a pistol on her and tried to take Amy." I put an arm around her shoulders. If I'd expected trembling or tears, I would have been disappointed.

"I didn't see a body," I said quizzically.

"He was still alive when we left him," Porsche said with a wicked grin. "He just wasn't interested in taking a girl with him." I made a pained face at the thought of where Maya must have put the bullet.

"We got here a couple of hours ago," Maya said, suddenly sounding as tired as I felt.

"Then you guys need to get some rack time," I said. "I'll keep an eye on things for a while, then I'll wake someone up to take over for me."

"What about you, baby?" Maya said. "You've been awake as long as anyone else, and you've been through a lot since yesterday."

"I was knocked out for a few hours," I said as I got to my feet. "Besides, there are a few things I want to do before I crash."

I got up and kissed Maya again for good measure, then headed for the windmill. Karl fell in step beside me.

"How did you afford this place?" he asked me. "I know your books made some money, but not that much."

"The books made more than you think, but Nate helped me finance it. Those two storage pods are his, the rest is mine."

"So, is this your survivalist retreat or something? Were you planning on sitting out the end of the world with a pile of guns and MREs?" He laughed as he asked the question, and I turned to face him.

"No, I'm not that kind of prepper. Most preppers aren't paranoid gun freaks waiting for the world to end. Look around you, what do you see? A little shack in the woods, a few outbuildings?"

"And an old windmill," Karl added with a grin.

"Here's what you don't see," I said with a wave of my hand. "That 'old windmill' pumps water, generates electricity and it's an antenna for a shortwave radio. That shed over there holds a series of deep cycle marine batteries to store the electricity the windmill generates, and my radio. That shed over there holds buckets of heirloom seeds and hand plows. Back there is twenty acres that used to be fields of wheat. Inside that little barn by the windmill with the solar panels on it is enough food to keep four people alive for a year. This isn't a survivalist retreat, Karl it's a homestead."

"We're just going to sit this out here?" he said. "Is that your big plan?" He raised his arms then let them drop to his side.

"No. For almost anything else, that would have worked but this...no." As I spoke, I went to the base of the windmill and grabbed the copper lead to the antenna. Most of the time, I kept the main antenna disconnected to keep the shortwave's effective range lower, but today none of that mattered. "We may be safe here for another day or so, but not much longer. I don't know if you saw it in the dark, but zombies are leaving the city."

"Why?" Karl asked, for once not challenging me.

"They're following the people; they're following their food." I connected the antenna lead and stood up to face him again. He'd gone a little pale and his eyes were vacant. Processing the idea that he wasn't at the top of the food chain anymore must have been hard for him. "Go get some rest, Karl," I told him. "I'm going to walk the fence line, make sure we don't have visitors, then I'll be back."

By the time I got back from my trip around our fence line, almost everyone was asleep. When I took a look inside the cabin, I found Cassie and Bryce in their sleeping bags on the floor of our little front room, with Karl sprawled out on the other side of the room, with an empty sleeping bag in between them. Maya and Amy's feet were visible in the loft bed, and Sherman was serving as a pillow for Leo in the little kitchen. All told, our little cabin wasn't much more than twenty feet on a side, but it served well enough for today. If we were staying here longer, I would have wanted to get a camper or two for the first winter.

Porsche was sitting at the picnic table with her cell phone in her hands. When she looked up at me, her face was longer than a Friday before a three day weekend. I sat across from her and leaned the Ruger against the table's edge.

"What's up?" I asked gently.

"I'm sorry I left you last night," she said slowly. "When you said go, the only thing I could think of was getting away."

"No, you did exactly what I needed you to do, Porsche," I told her. "You did the hardest thing anyone could have asked you to do. You left someone behind to save the rest of the people with you." She shook her head and her mouth turned down in distaste.

"Doesn't mean I like it," she muttered.

"No one's asking you to. But if you hadn't, they might have gotten Bryce and Cassie. There's no telling what would have happened to them then. So, you did good. I'm proud of you." Her expression brightened a little at that.

"Thanks," she said, still a little subdued. "So, what's next? This doesn't feel like our last stop."

"What makes you say that?" I asked her.

"You still have that same look on your face you had whenever we got to one of the places we were going. It's the same look you have when you get to work every day, and you're planning ahead for something."

"Okay, touché. This is just the first stop. I promise, I'll tell you everything soon, when I tell everyone else. As soon as I know what the plan really is. In the meantime, why don't you get some rest?"

She shook her head. "Not until you do. Maya has Amy watching out for her, you've got me. Deal with it." I looked at her for a moment, trying to see what I'd missed about the woman sitting in front of me. At work, she'd been a lot like anyone else. Her interests had seemed pretty much mainstream, though she hadn't been as obsessed with Hollywood gossip or reality TV as most of our co-workers. She'd had a couple of boyfriends that hadn't worked out, but I'd never heard her get vindictive about them, and she went out on weekends like anyone else, drank a little too much on occasion and lamented the fact on Monday mornings. On the surface, she was normal. The only thing that had made her stand out was that she would actually talk to me. She had never made fun of my geeky interests, and she even knew about some of the things I liked. Maybe that had been the first clue to what I was seeing here. When it had come down to it, she'd been willing to do what needed to be done. Hell, she'd driven into a horde of zombies to save my ass less than an hour after shit had truly started to hit the fan.

"Okay," I said. "Keep your ears open as much as your eyes. The fences should stop most undead a long ways from us so the road is pretty much the only approach for zombies. Other survivors are the biggest danger, and fences aren't going to slow them down much." She nodded and grabbed the M-4 from the bench beside her.

"You know how to use that?" I asked her.

"Maya showed me the basics. It's only got one clip for it though."

"Magazine," I corrected as I pulled two more from my vest and laid them on the table. "Clips are different. Take those. It'll do for now, but we need to get you better trained on it. And on the M9. We'll take care of that later. Right now, I need to get on the radio." She nodded and scooped up the two spare magazines and tucked them into her pockets.

I left her sitting at the table and headed for the electrical shed. Inside was a metal folding table that held my shortwave radio, a heavily modified Icom unit that I had picked up when I was still in the Air Force. Laid out at the back of the shed were the batteries that stored the power generated by the windmill and solar panels. I'd put a kerosene heater out here for use in the winter, and a single energy efficient light bulb set in the rafters so I could work at night. I pulled the folding metal chair out and sat down at the table, then pulled my code book from its hiding place under the table. As the set warmed up, I plugged in the continuous wave key, which was basically a Morse code tapper, and opened the code book.

One of the things Nate Reid and I had worked out months ago was a series of five letter codes that each had a specific meaning. Without the code book, they read as gibberish. I entered the frequency we had decided on, then reached for the key. It was time to reach out and touch someone.

I woke up when Maya kissed me. My eyelids felt like they were glued shut, and I didn't want to be awake, but there were these very soft lips against mine. Even sleep took second place to that. She giggled when I pulled her to me, and her lips went to my neck.

"Wake up sleepy head," she whispered.

"Wha' time izzit?" I mumbled.

"It's six. The natives are getting restless. And dinner's almost done." That got my eyes open and my stomach rumbling. Maya smiled at me from inches away and sat up. "You have enough time to grab a hot shower, if you hurry." I didn't need any more prodding. I followed her down the short ladder and stumbled to the bathroom. The small shower was big enough for one person, or two if you didn't mind it being a little tight, and the hot water heater was pretty efficient. The stream of warm water felt like magic on my skin, and I washed the sweat and grime of the past twenty four hours off of my body. Then I just stood there and let the heat soak through my muscles. When it finally started to cool off, I reluctantly shut it off and got dressed in a pair of sweats and a heavy sweatshirt. I emerged from the little bathroom feeling almost like a new person, though I still felt every bump and bruise from the journey out here.

The smell of beef stew hit my nose while I was putting my tennis shoes on in the front room, and I followed it to the kitchen, where Maya was stirring one of our large pots. She saw me coming and grabbed a bowl from the cabinet. Two ladles full of stew went into it, and she handed me the steaming bowl with a spoon before doling the same out to herself.

"Okay," she said to Amy. "Remember, two full ladles for everyone, no more. And no seconds unless I say so."

"I know, Mom," Amy said as she rolled her eyes. "This has to last us for Goddess knows how long, this is all we have 'til we grow our own." She quoted Maya in a tired voice as she grabbed a pair of potholders and picked up the bubbling pot of stew. We followed her out and sat at the table. One of our lanterns was lit and shedding a circle of light on the table. Someone had laid a fire in the firepit, and it was crackling gently, providing more light and some welcome heat against the evening's chill. More bowls were already stacked and waiting, and she served the stew out with exacting precision, even quelling her own father's rebellious look with a glare she had to have inherited genetically from her mother.

"This is all we have Dad," she said. "We have no idea how long we have to make it last."

"You didn't plan for this?" he asked me snidely.

"If he didn't, you're damned lucky he decided to let you come along!" Cassie said, her own voice sharp. "If it wasn't for them, you'd probably be dead right now. And my son and I would be locked in a cell or God knows what else. So do us all a favor and shut up." She sat down and turned her back to Karl, her bowl held in shaking hands. Bryce went to stand next to her, and he gave Karl hateful looks over his mother's shoulder.

"Is that it?" Karl said. "I'm lucky he allowed me to come along? So I'm just here on sufferance?"

"Both of you!" I snapped. "Stop. Rule twenty two. Watch out for your friends and family. That's why you're here, Karl. And no, I did *not* plan for this. I didn't plan for zombies and I didn't *plan* for having more people with us. But someone did. And as soon as we're done eating, I'll let you all in on the plan." I sat down and dug in to my food, my stomach sour.

"Way ta go, dad," Amy said as she sat down beside him. Porsche sat beside Cassie and nodded to Bryce, who sat across from her and started eating as well. For a few minutes, silence reigned. The stew was freeze-dried Mountain House, which was good on its own, but Maya always added some potatoes and bullion to bulk it up a little and add some stronger flavor to it. My spoon hit the bottom of the bowl too soon, both for my stomach's taste and my brain's. Maya, to my relief, forced Bryce and Amy to take seconds, and Karl didn't object, which I counted as a minor miracle. Finally, I couldn't put the moment off any longer.

"All right, boys and girls," I said as I got to my feet. The sun had faded from the sky, leaving the lantern and the fire as my only sources of light. Six pairs of eyes followed me as I went to the other side of the fire and tossed a log onto it. "First of all, we're not staying here. I got in touch with Nate today, and he gave me a location for us to meet him. He also gave me something else: the combinations to the locks on his storage sheds. Everything we need for the trip should be inside."

"You talked to my dad?" Bryce asked.

"Not exactly. It was all in Morse code. But he did ask about you and your Mom." I dug out the slip of paper I'd written the combination to one of the locks on and held it out to him. "Here, I think he'd like it if you opened up this one. I'll get the other one." We went to the two cargo containers. I directed Bryce to the one on the right, and I went to the other one. The heavy combination locks popped open and I pulled mine free, then lifted the bar and pulled the door to mine open. A set of fluorescent lights blinked on as I pulled the door wide, revealing the contents in all their glory. My jaw could have hit the floor.

Inside the shed was the bastard child of truck and an RV decked out in digital gray camo. It had the front end of a truck, but the back end was a compact camper, but it lacked the large windows and cab-over bed. The windshield and windows were covered with a metal meshwork that was large enough to see through easily but too small for more than two fingers to fit through it. The front was big enough to hold four passengers comfortably. I could see far enough into the back to see a small stove and sink on the driver's side. Storage lined the rest of what I could see. I looked over at Bryce to see what his reaction was.

"Wow!" he said as he stepped inside. I took a couple of steps over to see that the other shed had the same thing in it. Since they looked the same, I followed Bryce in and opened the passenger side door. From the inside, I could see that the vehicle also had room in the back for four single beds stacked two to a side. The driver's side seemed to be devoted to living arrangements, with the tiny stove and sink set over a small refrigerator, and the cabinets above and beside it devoted to pantry space. The largest door opened onto a toilet and a sink, then a tall, narrow door that opened onto a tiny closet. The passenger side was a mix of armory and survival gear, including a couple of tents and a folding table. The gun cabinet opened to reveal a rack that held two M-14s, two Ruger 10/22s and a pair of Remington 870 pump shotguns, with two M9s clipped to the door. Boxes of ammo were stacked in the bottom. Two drawers below that revealed cleaning kits and four knives. I smiled as I recognized the Aircrew Survival Egress Knife, or ASEK, that I had suggested to him instead of the usual Army M9 bayonet. The

155

ASEK was a better utility knife, and for civilian survival, it would do the same job as the bayonet, only much better.

While Bryce and Cassie explored their vehicle, I went back to the other shed. Amy was in the back, and Maya had climbed into the front passenger seat. "Look, honey, it even has a laptop up front," she said with a teasing smile.

"Great, I'll be able to write another book," I said.

"We should have grabbed some of our DVDs," Amy said from in back.

"Guess we'll have to stop at a Best Buy or something," Maya answered. I left them to explore and went to the back of the vehicle, noting the emblem on the back that read "Land Master Edition". There was a trailer hitch on the back and an extended storage deck. Karl and Porsche were waiting for me when I stepped out of the shed, neither of them looking happy.

"Where are we going exactly?" he demanded.

"To a place in southern Wyoming. Just west of Medicine Bow National Forest. Way off the beaten track, so there won't be so many dead people walking around."

"That's a plus," Porsche said. "So, what about all your stuff here? Seems like a lot to just leave behind." To my amazement, Karl nodded in agreement with her.

"You're right. We're going to have to load up as much as we can tonight. There's a trailer in the barn where we stored our food stock. We'll get as much as we can in it, and stow the bikes on the back of the Land Masters."

Cassie and I started up the Land Masters and pulled them out of the sheds, then we got the trailer hooked to the back of hers. I set half hour watches on the road, and we got to work. By ten o'clock, both vehicles were loaded and prepped. My shortwave radio ended up mounted in my Land Master, and the disassembled bike trailers ended up on the top racks. Finally, tired and sweaty, we all found ourselves gathered around the campfire with bottles of Heartland Ale for the adults and cups of

156

soda in the hands of Amy and Bryce. Sherman was lying at Porsche's feet and Leo had crawled up into the crook of my arm.

"You know what I'm going to miss?" Porsche said out of the blue. "Pizza." That got a few murmurs of agreement, especially from me.

"Soda," Bryce said, holding his cup up for emphasis.

"Mickey D's fries," Amy said.

"Breakfast cereal," Cassie chimed in.

"Chocolate," Maya said, and got a chorus of agreement.

"Ice," was my contribution.

"Toilet paper," Karl said. No one else said anything for a few moments as the depth of that one set in. Conversation picked back up a few minutes later, and more things we were going to miss came up, like the internet and hot showers. No one mentioned any of the people they were going to miss, and I didn't think it was a good idea to bring that up just then. Things were still too raw to start dwelling on the dead.

"Welcome to the new social networking, folks," I said as I gestured to the circle around the fire. "No more anonymous trolls, no more memes, just people talking. But, for us, it's late. We're going to have to get an early start in the morning." Everyone got up and headed off in one of two directions. Amy and Bryce wandered toward the Land Masters with Karl and Cassie behind them.

"You guys mind if I sleep on your floor tonight still?" Porsche asked with her head down and her eyes averted.

"Of course you can," Maya said with a smile, as if the answer was obvious. "I know that look. What are we going to be doing while everyone else is asleep?" she asked me after Porsche made it into the cabin. Any other night, it would have been filled with mischief and heat. Tonight, she sounded resigned.

"Planning our route. And listening to the airwaves. I get a funny feeling that I'm not going to like what I hear out there tonight."

157

"It's the zombie apocalypse honey," she reminded me. "What's to like?"

Truer words had rarely been spoken.

Chapter 13

The Color of Authority

No oppression is so heavy or lasting as that which is inflicted by the perversion and exorbitance of legal authority.
~ *Joseph Addison* ~

"It's a lot worse than I thought," I said as we all gathered around the Land Masters. "First, we have a new President, Gabriel Shaw, formerly known as the Secretary of Homeland Security. Secondly, President Shaw-"

"You mean Acting President Shaw," Karl interrupted.

"He didn't use that title," I corrected. "And yes, I know my civics. He's supposed to, but he's calling himself the President. But that's a minor thing compared to the rest. *President* Shaw has declared martial law, which I'm sure surprises everyone here. He's also declared that all US citizens are to report to regional processing centers for relocation to Designated Safe Zones. According to the radio broadcasts we heard last night, it's compulsory and failure to report is considered treason, and anyone who resists being rounded up for processing and relocation will be shot on sight. As an aside, looters will also be shot on sight."

"Well, damn," Cassie said drily. "There went my plans for the weekend." That got a laugh out of everyone, and I was grateful for the lift in the mood.

"More than you might think," I said as I looked around the group. "If we leave today, we'll all be in danger. Our own government might try to kill us. We have the supplies to last here for about a year, maybe longer if we hunt and scavenge. But I don't know if or when the infected will find us. What I do know is that they're already following the survivors out of Springfield." Everyone was quiet at that reminder, and I gathered my resolve for the next part. "As much as I hate to consider it, reporting for processing is still an option."

"No," Cassie said before I could continue. "For Bryce and me, that isn't even an option. You know that, Dave." She put an arm around Bryce's shoulders, and I could feel the heat of her anger across the five feet that separated us. "If the rest of you want to turn yourselves in, fine. I'd rather take my chances with running."

Porsche stepped forward with a grim look in her eyes. "No way. I'm not turning myself in."

"I'm not either," Maya said. "Not after what Dave told us." She turned a cold glare on Karl.

"For once, we agree on something, if for completely different reasons," he said as he raised his hands between them. It was half placating and half defense. "If DHS wants you for some reason, then they'll use Amy to get to you. My daughter is not a bargaining chip."

"Unless there's money involved," Maya spat.

"You're one to talk," Karl retorted.

"Mom! Dad!" Amy snapped. "Will you both please chill? God, you two are *so* immature. And by the way, I'm kinda right here, okay? And it's my life too. Not that I want to get 'processed' or anything," she turned to me. "I say we go, today." With her outburst, I turned to Bryce, who'd remained silent throughout the discussion.

"Bryce, what do you want to do? Stay or go?" I asked him.

"It's like Mom said," he offered in a voice barely above a whisper. "They want us. The zombies aren't the only ones who might come looking for us, are they?"

"Probably not," I said. "But I'm not sure. The DHS and the military pulled out of Springfield the same night we bugged out. Homeland is likely to be looking for us, but the military might not be."

"Then we'll be like the mages in Night of Fire," Bryce said, standing straighter. His voice lost the quiet tone, and he suddenly sounded much older. "They'll look for us whether we hide or run. All we can choose now is whether to give them a moving target, or a stationary one. I aim to give them the one that's harder to hit." I smiled as he quoted my first book.

"Couldn't have said it better myself," I said. "So, who else says we go today?" Four adults raised their hands. Amy had already made her opinion known, but she raised her hand, too. It made her the fifth adult to raise her hand in my eyes.

"Okay, then. Saddle up."

Karl ended up riding shotgun in Cassie's truck, and Maya took her place up front with me. Porsche and Amy alternated between the passenger seats and wandering into the back as we drove. I had the built in CB radio set to channel twenty three, since it seemed the quietest at the moment, and my shortwave set to scan. During the day, when signal propagation was weakest, I wasn't picking up much except on the military bands, and most of that was encrypted. We stayed on the smaller farm roads that paralleled US 44. The back roads kept us away from major groups of zombies, though we did run into a few. Well, run into is sort of an overstatement. We ran *over* a few. The Land Master's heavy bumper made short work of them, and the undercarriage's high clearance made sure we only felt a couple of bumps. But after the first ten miles, we ran into our first challenge. The road T'd ahead of us, the western route taking us right into Pleasant Hope, the right taking us miles out of our way before it turned north again. Instead of turning either way, I grabbed the pair of bolt cutters and got out of the truck. Tall grass rustled around my boots as I walked through it to the ancient, rusty barbed wire fence. With four quick snips, the wire pinged and coiled up on itself. We drove between the two fence posts and rambled across brown grass, angling toward a line of telephone poles that I was hoping led to the road on the other side of the field. Once we got across, all it took was another few snips, and we were rolling onto the road on the north side of the field and back on track. Our goal was to get north of Bolivar and take Highway 54 across Missouri 13, as close to midway between Springfield and Kansas City as we could get. On any other day, it would have been less than an hour's drive up 13

Highway to get there. On two lane roads that never seemed to go in a straight line for more than a few miles, it took us almost four hours to cover what would have been about fifty miles on the highway.

A little after one, we pulled up behind a stand of trees that blocked easy view of the highway. Everyone piled out, eager to stretch their legs after hours on their asses. The Land Masters were big and comfortable, but they were still a little cramped, especially for two teenagers.

"Everyone stay between the trucks and the trees," I called out.

"Ease up, Dave," Karl said, his tone dismissive. "There's no one around to see us."

"And what if you're wrong?" I asked as I headed for the sparse grass on the side of the road.

"Then we'll see them coming from a long ways off," he said, shaking his head. "And Maya says I have control issues." Amy and Bryce were huddled in front of Maya and Porsche as they handed out sandwiches, bags of chips and the increasingly prized soda.

Cassie came up beside me, her hands on her hips as she tried to stretch her back out. "So, we cross the highway here and head for Kansas, right?" she said more than asked. I nodded and we headed for the edge of the trees. The road was empty and the air was still. There was quiet and then there was total silence, and we had the latter going on. Even the breeze seemed reluctant to get near the road.

"No cars on the road here," I observed. "That's good. If we can make it to Kansas, we should be able to make it to Nebraska or Colorado pretty easily, and from there, into Wyoming."

"Not into Colorado. Everything from Fort Collins down to Castle Rock is one big city." I looked at her and nodded, filing that part away. "I grew up in Boulder," she said.

"Then I guess we're heading up into Nebraska," I said.

162

"Do you hear that?" Cassie asked as we turned to head back.

"No, I don't hear an-" I started to say, then stopped as the low *whup-whup-whup* of rotor blades reached my ears. "Everyone down! Don't move!" I yelled as I threw myself flat on the ground. I started counting, and when I got to thirty, a pair of Blackhawks flew overhead. For a moment, I was afraid we'd been spotted, but they didn't turn around. Instead, they went maybe another mile down the road, then I could hear the steady pounding of a heavy gun. I risked standing up, and saw tracers streaking from the choppers to the ground as they circled something. Cassie and I sprinted back to the trucks and crouched next to everyone else.

"What are they doing?" Amy asked.

"Probably shooting at zombies," I told her. I gave Karl a meaningful look, but he wasn't impressed by me being right.

"Or survivors," Porsche added. After a few minutes, the choppers moved on, leaving columns of smoke in their wake as they headed further north. Everyone moved when I did, and moments later we had the trucks started up and on the road again. For another half hour, we navigated over more two-lane asphalt, tracking as far north and south as we did west. Even in October, Missouri was green and beautiful, with most trees not showing their fall color yet. Since it was still in the first days of fall, it was warm enough for me to drive with the window down if I kept my sweatshirt on. And after the choppers had almost flown up on us, I wanted to be able to hear as much as I saw. The low hum of the engine and the hiss of the tires on the asphalt were the only sounds. The shortwave was set on scan, and it hadn't been very active. Even the birds seemed to be wary of drawing attention to themselves. Amy had opted to sit on the floor so Sherman could press his nose against the wire grill of the passenger side rear window, while Porsche sat in the seat behind me. Maya was riding shotgun beside me. Only she was carrying a pistol instead of a scattergun. Of course, so was I. Everyone on board was armed, with Amy's pink Ruger stashed behind her seat. My HK assault rifle was stashed behind my seat, sharing space with my survival tube.

We all jumped when the shortwave squawked. "Billy!" a high pitched male voice called out. "I got two big campers or somethin' down on thirty-two, just past Wright Cemetery. Look pretty nice, and they got women with 'em."

"How many men?" another voice demanded. This one was deeper and more controlled, with less of the Missouri softening of his vowels.

"I only see one. I got 'im in my sights. You want me to take him out?"

"Don't be stupid. You're not gonna hit a moving target at that kinda range. Walt'll get 'em at ninety-seven junction. You got that, Walt?"

"I got 'em," a voice I guessed was Walt's answered.

"Fuck!" I spat as I grabbed the microphone for the CB and keyed it to transmit. "Cassie, stay close and don't stop unless I do. We have some trouble heading our way."

"Copy," Cassie said. I stepped on the gas and felt the Land Master surge forward. The road sign said that the junction with Missouri 97 was about a mile ahead, and the truck hit sixty in nothing flat.

"Porsche, grab a shotgun from the gun cabinet and get it loaded. If we stop, Maya and I will cover the front, I want you to get out behind us and keep an eye on our six o'clock. Amy, put Sherman in the back and tie his leash off. If things go bad, you get behind the wheel and get the hell out, you got it?" I checked the rearview mirror in time to see her nod, her eyes wide and round. A few thugs wouldn't have worried me, but they were using the police bands, which meant they'd probably show up in police *cars* and if they were broadcasting with a local police department's tower, then odds were good they could be picked up by any decent radio direction finder in the western half of the state. Assholes with police equipment but no police training, I could handle. Trained troops in Blackhawks were a different story.

164

Maya pulled her pistol and worked the slide to chamber a round, and I followed suit, putting my knee against the wheel to free my right hand to pull the slide back on my Colt before I reholstered it. She pulled up the map on the laptop and stared at it for a moment. A slow, wolfish smile spread across her face and she turned to me.

"Take the left for Old Ninety-Seven Highway," she said, pointing up ahead of me. I looked up ahead. The road curved to the right, but I could also see a smaller road that kept going straight. As the turn off got closer, I saw a police cruiser parked in the middle of the road with a man standing behind it. I braked and pulled the truck across the left lane and onto the gravel road that connected Highway 32 with 97. The Land Master rocked with the change in the road's pitch and gravel crunched under the tires as I pulled the wheel hard to the right to make the dog-leg. The back end slewed out behind me and I hit the gas again, spraying gravel. Cassie pulled in behind me and closed the gap between us. Over the radio I could hear Walt screaming that we'd gotten past him and calling Billy and Jim to help him chase us down. I heard sirens behind us and saw flashing blue and red lights as we closed on 97. The truck skidded through the left turn, then we were speeding down 97. We took the first left and stayed on 97, headed for another small road that would take us south of Nevada. By the time we were turning west onto the road we wanted, I could see three of the white cruisers behind us, and they were gaining on Cassie's truck. I keyed the mic again.

"Cassie, take the lead. Stay on E!" I called out as I pulled into the left lane. Her truck surged ahead when I hit the brakes again, then there was a police cruiser pulling up on my right. I saw the driver's window start to roll down. Maya shifted her pistol to her left hand and fired through the mesh. The cruiser slowed enough to drop behind the windows, so I braked and swerved hard right. Metal screeched when I hit it, and the truck shuddered for a moment, then the cruiser was plowing through barbed wire fence. The moment I was in the right lane, the second cruiser sped past me and rocketed toward Cassie's Land Master. The third cruiser swerved into the rear quarter panel on my side, but it simply didn't have the mass to do more than make me swerve a little. I stomped on the gas and left it behind momentarily as I bore down on his partner. I caught up to him as he pulled even with Cassie and rammed his rear bumper hard enough to move him ahead of her. I hit him again and he made the mistake of trying to get out of my way. When I rammed him a third time, my front bumper clipped the left side of his bumper and he shot across to the right side of the road and started to spin out. Cassie dropped back and avoided him and we left him behind in a cloud of dust. The traffic over the radio was turning the air blue, and I was tempted to join them as I heard the sound I'd been dreading: rotors. I checked my outside rear view mirror and saw flashing lights and shadows on the road behind me. Then I felt the chop of rotor wash and saw a Blackhawk drop down in front of me. The big chopper turned sideways and I found myself staring into the barrels of a mini-gun.

I hit the brakes and pulled in front of Cassie to make sure she got the message to stop. She pulled to a stop a few yards behind me. For a few seconds, the tableau held, then I heard the Blackhawk's PA system.

"Exit your vehicles with your hands behind your heads," the lead Blackhawk boomed.

"What do we do?" Amy asked.

"What he says," I said dejectedly as I pulled my pistols and dropped them on the floorboard. I picked up the mic again. "Everyone disarm and get out." I opened the door and put my hands out where they were visible and stepped out. The other doors opened and everyone else followed suit. I laced my fingers together behind my head and stepped clear of the truck. Ropes dropped from the chopper's doors and eight men in dark green camo slid down. *Marines,* I found myself thinking as they approached us with their assault rifles up.

"Turn around!" one of them yelled. "Walk backward toward us! Now!" Even Karl obeyed without a word. When we got closer to them, the lead Marine barked "On your knees, now!" One by one, we went to our knees. I heard the sound of boots and gear rattling as they approached us. Behind us, I could see the three cruisers approaching. A second and third chopper

166

flanked the road, one higher than the other. The lower bird opened fire with a sharp burp, and I could hear the bullets hit the pavement in a series of pops. The cruisers ignored the gunfire and kept coming.

"Contact front!" one of the Marines called out, and I heard eight guns coming up and charging handles being pulled.

"Stop your vehicles and get out!" the PA system on the chopper that had fired the first shots called out. Evidently, the dumbasses in the cars had watched one too many movies where the terrorists killed soldiers by the dozen simply because they were willing to shoot first. The cars pulled to a stop and the doors burst open. Two men jumped out of each cruiser and brought their weapons up, but none of them got so much as a single shot off. M-16s popped and chattered behind us and the Blackhawks cut loose with their mini-guns. I could hear the thugs' all too brief screams amid the metallic pops of bullets turning the cars into Swiss cheese as they flopped like rag-dolls and fell to the ground.

"Hold your fire! Hold your fire!" someone called out, and others took up the call. Suddenly, there was just the sound of brass tinkling to the ground and the fading echoes of gunfire.

"Reloading!" someone called out. Seconds later, another Marine followed suit, and another, until all eight had fresh magazines in.

"Kaminski! Blake! Clear the cars." Two Marines jogged forward as two others spread out to the side of the road.

"Have you had any contact with the infected?" the lead Marine barked out again. "Have any of you been bitten?"

"No one's been bitten," I answered. "No direct contact with the infected. Just shot a bunch of 'em." I heard movement behind me and another Marine spoke nearby, his voice barely audible to me over the rotorwash.

"Ma'am, please put your hands behind your back for me," he said to Maya. Moments later, I heard the distinctive rasp of a zip tie being pulled closed, then another. "This is just a precaution. We'll take them off once we're sure you haven't been exposed. Alright, I'm going to help you stand up, now." The process was repeated with everyone else. The other two choppers landed, and I watched Maya being loaded on to one.

"Take the vest off," the Marine behind me ordered me. I undid the fasteners and pulled the vest off. Another man came up and grabbed it, then I was pushed to the ground face first and my hands were pulled behind my back and bound together. One Marine held me in place while another searched me; he emptied my pockets and frisked me thoroughly, and not gently. Once he was sure I wasn't hiding any bombs or guns, I was pulled to my feet and frog-marched toward the chopper across the road from the one Maya had been loaded into.

At the door to the chopper, I found myself face to face with the leader, a tall lieutenant with deep brown skin and eyes that looked like he was inches away from a thousand yard stare. "Are my men going to find any surprises in your vehicles?" he asked me.

"A big Rottweiler and an orange attack cat," I said conversationally. "Be careful around the cat. He's very territorial." That got a smile out of him for about a microsecond.

"Don't worry. Your pets will be taken good care of, sir," he said. The lieutenant ordered two of his men, Lee and Simmons, to drive the trucks back to base, then I was hustled onto the chopper and ended up sitting across from Karl and Amy. The other two choppers lifted off as we did and turned north, then banked west after a few minutes.

Once we got some altitude, I could see columns of black smoke rising from the landscape below us, and a wall of dark clouds to the south. North of us, I could see thicker columns of smoke rising in the distance. One of the Marines noticed where I was looking and nudged my shoulder.

"Know what that is?" he asked. I shook my head and he continued. "That's Kansas City. Whole fucking city's burning." We started to descend a few seconds later, and I got my first glimpse of their base. A heavy iron fence surrounded the edge of the airport, and infected were pressed against the eastern side.

Another fence surrounded the airfield. Five hangars were in an uneven line stretching southeast from the main building, with a big concrete pad north of them that stretched in a thick L around the end of the northern edge of the main terminal, which was a square two story metal structure. A couple of newer looking buildings sat to the west of the hangars and terminal. Seven Blackhawks and a four C-130s sat in a row on the concrete pad, and a walled compound had been built south of the runway. Another C-130 was parked at the north end of the runway, and a Chinook sat behind it on the grass. Our flight of choppers circled the airfield to the north and came to rest on the runway as four Humvees pulled up, two with machine guns mounted in turrets on the top.

"Welcome to FOB Nevada," the lieutenant yelled over the noise of the chopper's rotors as he hopped down onto the tarmac. "We'll get you inprocessed and get you out of those zip-strips as soon as we can, and we'll have you on the first plane we can out of here. This time tomorrow, you'll be in a safe zone." They led us to one of the Humvees and helped us inside.

"This is the most courteous violation of my civil rights I've ever seen," Karl muttered as we rode toward the walled compound.

"We can't take chances with peoples' safety, sir," one of the Marines in the back with us said. I nodded and gave Karl a pointed look. His face looked like he'd just swallowed a lemon, but he shut up. A couple of minutes later, we pulled up at the compound. Again, the Marines helped us out and led us through a heavy metal door. Inside, we found ourselves in a long corridor with plexiglass panels in the upper half of the walls. Karl and I were motioned to the left by two men in blue hazmat suits while Amy was taken to the right by a woman in a yellow suit. They led us into separate rooms, and the man with me cut the zip strips off my hands before he told me to disrobe. The room itself was pretty bare, with only a metal exam table and a stool. I laid my clothes on the exam table as I took them off and turned to look at the man with me once I was down to my underwear.

169

"Please remove everything, sir," he said firmly. I slid them down and laid them on the table then turned around.

"Try not to be too intimidated or anything," I said in my best deadpan.

"Subject displays bruising over the majority of the torso," the man said as he stepped up close to me and reached for my right arm. "Including abrasions on both wrists consistent with having the hands bound. No bite marks on the arms, chest, neck or back. Please sit on the table, sir." I put my bare butt on the metal and felt my ass cheeks clench from the cold steel against them. "Legs bear some scratch marks consistent with movement through brush. No parallel scratches. Bruise consistent with a bite mark on the right ankle, coloration indicates the wound is at least twenty four hours old. No scabbing or indications that skin was broken. Were you bitten by one of the infected, sir?"

"Gummed," I said seriously. "It didn't have any teeth. That happened Monday night."

"Okay. Looks like you're clear. What is your name sir?"

"Dave Stewart," I answered, seeing no reason to lie to him. Even if I'd wanted to, odds were pretty good that I wouldn't get away with it. He told me to get dressed again, and escorted me down the hallway to another room. This one had a one way mirror on the far wall and bubbles for cameras. A door was set in the wall to the right of the one I'd been led in through, and as soon as I sat down at the plain table, it opened to let a Marine lieutenant in. He tossed my vest and the two challenge coins onto the table before he sat down across from me.

"Care to tell me how you came to have these?" he said as he laid a file folder on the table. "Not to mention a Special Forces issue sidearm and a government issue assault rifle in your possession."

"It's been an interesting couple of days," I said.

"I've got time. Tell me about it," he said, his voice level. I hit rewind for him and described my journey out of town in as much detail as I could without revealing Nate or his role in the plan. I could tell the lieutenant was skeptical of the whole story,

170

but hey, we were in the middle of the zombie apocalypse. How much weirder could my story get?

"And then your guys saved our asses from those guys in the cop cars," I finished.

"And Colonel Shafer will verify your story," he said, his tone saying what he wasn't: *bullshit.*

"Well, the part about the stadium, sure," I told him. I read the name tape about his right breast pocket. "Look Lieutenant Parker, I know it sounds weird, but it's true."

"Let's go back to how you ended up at the MSU operating base. You said they captured you. Why?"

"Like I said, they had orders to. I don't know why, and they didn't tell me. The agent in charge tried to order them to kill me, but they refused it as an unlawful order. I don't know if they were looking for me in particular or if they were just looking for someone to take in. Maybe they needed to round up a left handed man."

"And once you helped them get out of the stadium, they didn't try to take you prisoner again." We danced like that for another hour, with him asking me to repeat parts of the story or clarify things. Making a subject repeat their story was a standard interrogator's tactic, designed to uncover the inconsistencies inherent in a lie. Since I wasn't lying, there wasn't much for me to screw up. Finally, he stood up and picked up the vest. "You can keep the challenge coins. Come with me, and we'll take care of the rest of your personal property." He led me out the door he came in, and I found myself in a room with a desk and a bored looking Marine behind it.

"We're confiscating your vehicles, Mr. Stewart," the Marine behind the desk said. "You'll be compensated for them at a fair value to be determined later. That includes the weapons on board and all the contents. Your animals will be boarded and the cost taken out of your compensation for the vehicles and other personal property. Civilians aren't allowed to possess firearms in the safe zones. Do you understand the situation as I've described it to you?"

"Understand it, yes. Consent to it, no."

"We're not asking for your consent, sir. You'll be on the first flight out to the St Louis safe zone tomorrow morning. Head out through the door to your left and you'll find the rest of your family waiting." He gestured toward the door. I went through it, fuming and cursing the fake cops for giving our position away to the military. The open area I found myself in was surrounded by high concrete walls with walkways near the top. A mess tent was set up to the right with an open dining fly next to it, and another dozen tables out in the open. On the left side of the yard were more tents, and judging by the way people were wandering in and out of them, I was guessing they were temporary quarters. On the far side was a set of port-o-potties and crude showers. Marines in full battle rattle were on the walls and near a set of large vehicle doors on the far side of the yard, as well as a few in utility uniforms and the distinctive eight point utility covers walking around the yard itself. Maya's voice called my name, and I found everyone else sitting at a table out in the open with tin mess trays in front of them.

"You're just in time for lunch," Maya said as I approached the table. "Go get something to eat, babe." She didn't need to tell me twice, especially since all of our food had just been confiscated. I headed into the tent and grabbed a tray, then shuffled along the line. I emerged with my tray laden with a hunk of meatloaf, mashed potatoes, green beans, two rolls and a bottle of water. I grabbed the spot next to Maya and put an arm around her for a moment before I dug in.

"It looks like we're all being sent to the safe zone in St Louis," Karl said as he pushed his tray away. "And as pleasant as they're trying to make the option sound, I still don't like it."

"Me, either," I said. "They took the trucks and all our stuff." That brought a round of cursing from everyone, even Bryce.

"Dad got that gun for me," he said. I shook my head to forestall further talk as I saw a Marine in a woodland pattern utility uniform heading for our table with a tray in his hands. He stopped in front of Porsche and looked over at us with a broad smile.

"You gentlemen looked a little outnumbered," he said. "I thought I'd even the odds a little, if you didn't mind the company."

"No, that's fine," Porsche said quickly. She gestured at the seat across from her and ran her hand through her hair.

"I'm Lance Corporal Porter," he introduced himself as he sat down. "You can call me Mike, though." Porsche gushed her name, and he pretty much ignored every other name that came his way after that.

"Mike, I noticed you guys seem to have no problem fraternizing with us civilians," I said. "Doesn't that make your CO nervous?"

"When we're off duty, he's got no problem with it," he said without losing a single watt of smile power. "You folks aren't prisoners; you're US citizens, just like us." He would have said more, but any conversation was drowned out by the drone of a C-130 taking off. It rose into sight over the wall, and I did a double take. I'd expected to see an olive drab plane grabbing sky, but this one was black, with gray tail numbers and no military blazon on its side or tail. I went to say something to him and found myself having to wait as a black Chinook went overhead.

"Now those DHS pukes," he pointed with his fork, "they didn't like mixing with civilians. I'm glad they're leaving."

"They're leaving?" Porsche said.

"Yeah," Porter said. "I think that was the last of 'em that just took off. Hell, you couldn't get one of those lily white bastards to get near the fence, either. My lieutenant hated 'em. He always had this fancy way of calling 'em chickenshit." He dropped his voice and screwed up his face into a distasteful expression. "Those DHS agents are the most risk averse sonsabitches I've ever seen." Porsche laughed at the impression, and everyone else gave it at least a smile. The thing was, after seeing a group of them leave Captain Adams team to a group of ghouls, I had to agree with him. And that was the thing about the "risk averse" crowd. Cowards usually had a highly developed

173

sense of danger. Any place they were leaving en masse was usually about to be the proverbial sinking ship.

"Then maybe we ought to be asking ourselves why they're in such a big rush to leave," I said.

"Probably the same reason we are," Porter said. "Too many infected piling up at the fence. We're pullin' out in the morning, too." I shut up and concentrated on eating while Porter regaled Porsche with stories about the things other refugees had brought with them. As he described a woman's desperate attempt to justify her collection of vibrators as essential, I wanted to snap at him. Talking about other peoples' hang ups was pointless. I wanted him gone from the table. Hell, the more I thought about it, the more pissed off I found that I really was. I wanted my vehicles back. I wanted my guns. Even being deprived of my sword felt like an insult. More than anything, I resented being locked inside this compound. With my stuff, I was more than capable of surviving outside on my own. I'd practically walked from the center of Springfield to my house near the edge of town, and made another fifteen miles on a bike. Forcing me to sit behind these walls and depend on the protection of someone else felt was demeaning.

Maya's touch was like a bucket of cold water being poured over my head, and I was suddenly aware of my heart hammering beneath my ribs and the metallic tang of an adrenaline rush in my mouth. "Baby, are you okay?" she whispered to me. "You look like you want to rip someone's head off." I turned to look at her and felt my jaw unclench as I blinked and struggled to get my bearings.

"I did," I said softly. "And this isn't the first time I've felt that. I got the same feeling when I was locked up at MSU with Patient Zero."

"Before Monday, I would have said that was impossible," she said. "Today, not so much."

"Corporal," I said when Porter paused for a second to take a breath. "Could you do me a favor and go up on the wall to see how bad the infected are getting? It would really put my mind at ease." Porsche looked my way, then bit her lip and smiled at Porter.

"Me, too," she said. I chuckled at him as he agreed to it and hustled off. When he got to the wall and started looking east, another Marine in combat gear joined him, and they pointed at something. Moments later, another Marine joined them and brought a pair of binoculars up. I looked behind me to see other Marines starting to look to the south and west. Then Porter was leading another Marine with sergeant stripes toward the table and pointing me out.

"Sir, please come with me," the sergeant said in a tone that meant it was not just a polite request, no matter how it sounded.

"You just can't stay out of trouble, can you?" Karl said without the usual contempt in his tone.

"Guess not. Gotta go to the principal's office. I'll be back," I said. I looked to Maya and tried to tell her with my eyes what I wanted to say out loud: *be ready.* I followed the two men back into the office area I'd so recently left and found myself standing in the interrogation room, face to face with a major in combat gear with as much silver as black in his high and tight buzz cut.

"Stewart," the major said in a tone usually reserved for ex-wives, butterbar lieutenants and other less desirable life forms. "How does a former wing-nut know what the infected are doing?" he demanded.

"Experience," I told him. "I saw the DHS boys bugging out. Last time I saw them move that fast was when their base in Springfield was about to be overrun. And…you might find this hard to believe, major, but I think they brought something…*someone* with them. A kind of zombie that can attract other zombies, maybe even control them."

"I do not believe this bullshit!" the major barked. "Sergeant, why in the hell are you wasting my time with this?"

"The number of infected on the eastern fence has nearly doubled, sir," the sergeant said. "And they're on all sides of the perimeter now."

175

"How did we miss that shit?" he demanded. The sergeant's reply was cut off when another man entered the room.

"Sir, the front gate just sent a runner," the new man said breathlessly. "They're reporting increasing numbers of infected."

"Why didn't they radio that shit in?" the major said with a look at me that said he clearly thought this was all my fault somehow.

"Radio trouble, sir."

"Well isn't that goddamn convenient? Alright, Klein, get the C-130s prepped to go ASAP. If those two confiscated trucks aren't loaded up yet, leave 'em. We're evacing on the double. Porter, gear up and lead a squad to the building those Homeland assholes headquartered out of. If you find what Stewart says you will, I wanna know about it pronto. If you don't, then you have my express permission to put your boot up his ass. Well, what're ya waitin' for? Move!"

All three Marines in the room called out "Oorah!" in unison and hustled out of the room, leaving me with the major.

"As for you, Stewart," the major said gruffly. "I have never in my entire life wanted a man to be wrong as bad as I do right now. Now get the hell out of my sight and try not to stir up any more goddamn trouble."

"No promises," I said as I turned and left the room.

Chapter 14

Choices

Love is not a feeling of happiness. Love is a
willingness to sacrifice.

~Michael Novak ~

As it turned out, one of the hardest things I had to do in the first days of the zombie apocalypse…was nothing. After almost two days of fighting, traveling and surviving, I discovered that I didn't handle waiting very well. Add into that the constant low level irritation I'd been feeling since we'd arrived, and I wasn't fit company for anyone I liked. Maya had left me be, and had slowly led the rest of the group to another table. People milled around in the compound's yard in little groups, some quiet, some loud, and a couple making a nuisance of themselves. An upstanding looking young man in all the latest Patagonia outdoor wear was facing off with the Marines at the vehicle gate. Behind him, an equally upstanding looking woman in a designer blouse and high end pants and hiking boots was talking over him at the same time. As I watched, the man turned and yelled at his wife, then turned back to the three Marines he had been trying to shout into submission.

"That isn't going to end well, is it?" Karl said as he sat on the table beside me.

"Nope," I said, shaking my head. "Any second now, that high class young man is going to say the wrong thing, and he's going to get a face full of pissed off Marine." As if on cue, the man made a move and ended up on his hands and knees puking. As the well-dressed man threw up at the Marine's boots, he stepped back. The woman with him retreated a few steps, looking suddenly less impressed with herself than she had been a few minutes before.

"That was…illuminating," Karl said as the sergeant ordered another Marine to help the man up.

"You could say that. The absolute last serviceman or woman you want to get in a fistfight with is a Marine," I said. Outside the compound, I could hear the sound of turboprop engines approaching.

"Duly noted. You know, there's a compound like this one in Springfield. I had to settle on a workman's comp claim for a construction worker who got hurt on the job there last year." He sounded disgusted.

"*You* took a settlement? Maya said you *never* take settlements."

"I never take a case I don't think I can win at trial," Karl corrected. "Settlements cut down on fees and hours billed, and I only got a percentage of a much smaller payout. When I took the case, I thought I was going to be facing off with FEMA or Department of Homeland Security. As it turned out, I ended up taking on Monos."

"Monos Incorporated? The company that makes…well, everything?" I asked incredulously. "That must have been like David and Godzilla," I joked.

"That's an accurate analogy," he said with a humorless smile. "The settlement was very generous, but given all the clauses they threw in, it had to be. Confidentiality, non-disparagement, even an indemnity clause. Hell, they even tried to make me sign a clause saying I'd never be a part of legal action against them again, but that happened after the settlement."

"Was the place in Springfield exactly like this one?" I asked as a growing suspicion started to edge into my mind.

"I don't know. I was never allowed inside. The only section my client saw was the one he worked on. But it looked a lot like this one on the outside, and it had the same kind of fences we saw when they brought us in. I wonder, though…how many more of these could there be?"

"How many regional processing centers are there?" I countered. "Does it seem to you like someone knew this was going to happen?"

"You were pretty well prepared," Karl said.

"Most of that was Nate helping me along, but point taken. Still, Monos, the company that makes everything from seeds to pesticides to whole brands of foods is helping build places like this," I said as I gestured to the thirty foot walls around us. "And guess where Monos moved their headquarters to three years ago. St Louis. Too many coincidences for my taste. Not that I can do much about it now."

"It looks like we're going to be able to find out for sure soon. Look, Dave, no matter what else happens I wanted to thank you for everything you've done. I know we haven't gotten along in the past. But the past couple of days, I've gotten the chance to get to know you better, and I think I misjudged you." Karl sounded like he was working really hard to get those words out, and it earned him a lot of respect.

"Thanks, Karl. I really ought to have said the same thing a couple of days ago. You put Amy first, in front of your own pride. It takes a hell of a man to do that. And if you ever mention this conversation in front of Maya, I will deny saying that completely."

"Likewise," he said with a nod. Another set of turboprops roared past, and I could hear the rise and fall in pitch that told me a plane was turning around. My guess was that the Corporal Porter had found exactly what I was afraid he would, and the evacuation was going even further ahead of schedule than the major said.

"Ladies and gentlemen, when your name is called, move to the exit and check in with the man there. Abrams, Jennifer." A young woman in a blue dress raised her hand and started toward the smaller personnel door. Maya led the rest of our group over to us as the first few names were called off. I did a headcount of the civilians in the compound and came up with a little more than a hundred, and that was more a wild ass guess than anything. I'd flown on a C-130 Hercules into and out of Iraq, and I knew they could carry almost a hundred people if that was all they were carrying. Add in gear, and that number dropped by about a third. Seventy people, plus stuff, would make one C-130 pretty cramped. I had no idea how many Marines were here, either. The logistics was beginning to give me a headache.

Then the screams started outside, and things like logistics and reason went out the window. At first, there was the strange stillness as people tried to figure out what was going on. Then the first gunshots sounded, and panic erupted. Even ten people trying to get out a single door was a recipe for disaster before you added in zombies. Ten times that number was like a meat grinder. Even I wanted to get out of the compound, though I knew our best bet was to stay inside the walls. I tried yelling for Maya and Amy, but the screaming drowned my voice out so completely I couldn't hear myself as I fought against the tide of bodies pushing me toward the narrow doorway. I caught a glimpse of Maya not ten feet away amid the throng, but it might as well have been ten miles between us for all that I could move against the crush of humanity around me. Then I saw Amy only a couple of feet away from me, and I reached out for her. Her hand closed around mine and I held on for dear life.

Suddenly, the pressure eased a little and she ended up in my arms. I would have gone down if it wasn't for the hand that caught my belt and dragged me back upright. Craning my neck, I saw Karl behind me, one hand on my shoulder, the other supporting Amy. In front of us, I could see the main doors swinging open as the human stampede pushed against them. The force of the people behind us propelled us out into the grass, and then we were pressed sideways as the mob turned toward the planes. The rear ramp of the plane in front was down, and everyone raced for it. It was a miracle no one ran into one of the rear plane's propellers. I looked toward the southern fence line and fought down a sense of panic as I saw the first group of ghouls racing toward us at the same time as I heard the engines of the front plane change pitch.

He's about to take off! I thought. I pointed at the rear plane and leaned that way, and Karl nodded, then let go of me to point over our heads at our destination. The mob was easier to move through going sideways than to fight its forward momentum, but we still had to struggle. Maya pulled Cassie free of the mass, and Porsche dragged Bryce free. They spared a look over their shoulders at us, but Karl waved them on as we fought our way toward the edge of the crowd. They sprinted toward the aft hatch of the second plane even as the first one started to surge forward. Its ramp had already started to come up, but people were still jumping on it until it pulled clear. Behind us, I could hear gunfire, but I didn't dare look. We were still fifty yards from the last plane, and we weren't the only ones headed for it any more. Like a flock of birds, the other twenty or so people turned as one and ran for the plane. Porsche shoved Bryce through the hatch, then turned and helped Maya get Cassie inside. For a moment, it looked like Maya was going to wait, but Porsche shoved her forward, too. With a look at me, she jumped in behind her. My feet pounded against the concrete of the runway.

Thirty yards left to go, and the plane started to pull forward as more and more people tried to get through the hatch. Porsche's face appeared in the door and she started pulling people on board.

Twenty yards away, and the plane was picking up speed, but I was still gaining. I grabbed Amy's hand and tried to make my feet go faster.

Ten yards, and we were keeping up with it.

Eight yards as I put on a final burst of speed, then it started to pull away. Maya's face appeared at the hatch, and she reached back for us, her face a mask of anguish as the plane gathered speed. Porsche and Cassie pulled her back in as the distance started to open between us and the door started to close. Then, as hope began to fade, something dropped from the hatch and tumbled along the tarmac. I slowed to a stop as the transport's nose came up, then the big bird's body lifted into the air.

"Mooooommm!" I finally heard Amy scream. I turned to look over my shoulder to see Karl jogging up behind us. Yards behind him a group four of Marines were trotting along. One stopped and turned, then fired a burst into the group of infected that were running toward them. Three ghouls dropped, but the zombies just kept moving. The Marine turned and sprinted forward, and as he passed the last man in the line, that man turned and did the same thing. Two more ghouls hit the pavement, and he turned and sprinted forward.

"Come on, pumpkin," Karl panted as he gathered Amy up. "No time to cry. Need to keep moving." Sweat poured down his face, and it took everything he had to speak, but he pulled her forward, and she followed, sniffling and sobbing. I picked my feet up as well. The Marines were headed for somewhere specific, and they had a plan. More importantly, they were armed. We stumbled along, trying to keep pace with them, and one of them pointed at something ahead of them as they passed us. Hope flared in my heart again as I saw their destination: three Blackhawk's, waiting about three hundred yards away, their rotors already turning. Marines were running toward them from the airport's main terminal, some of them turning to fire behind them. Karl swerved away from us for a moment and grabbed something from the runway, then came jogging back with my bug-out cache tube slung over his shoulder. I risked a glance behind us, and decided not to do that again. Behind us, hell, all around us, zombies and ghouls were closing in. As Karl fell back in with Amy and me, one of the Blackhawks lifted into the air, and a handful of Marines ran to the next one in the line. Moments later, it lifted off. By now, we were only yards away, and my lungs were burning. My legs felt like lead, and my throat felt like I'd swallowed hot coals. Several Marines were already on board, and the rear of the chopper started to look crowded. I pulled Amy forward, suddenly afraid they were going to take off without us. Hands reached out for us and I pushed Amy into them. There was barely enough room for Karl and me to perch on the edge of the rear deck, but camo clad arms reached out and linked with ours, holding us as secure as they could. Someone shouted to the pilot, and the Blackhawk's engine revved as it rose into the air. Below us, the dead converged, and we left them reaching up for us. I breathed a sigh of relief as the chopper's engines whined, then caught it as we started to slide sidewise.

"We're too heavy!" one of the Marines yelled, his voice barely audible over the noise of the engine and the rotors. "We have to dump some weight!" I looked over my shoulder at Amy, then at Karl, and we both knew what had to be done. I pushed against someone's shoulder and struggled to get to my feet, only to find Karl pushing me back.

"Don't be stupid!" I yelled at him as the chopper started to lose altitude. "You're her father. She needs you!" He pulled the cache tube off his shoulder and pushed it against me.

"You're her best chance to survive!" he screamed back at me. "Now swallow your goddamn pride and take care of my little girl!"

"Daddy, no!" Amy screamed as he reached out and put his hand to her face for a moment. She clutched at his hand, her knuckles white as she tried to hang on to her father. He leaned back, and I watched as his weight slowly pulled her arms straight, then his fingertips slipped free of hers, and he fell. Time stretched out around me as he dropped, seeming to fall forever toward the sea of the dead below us. Then, he disappeared into the horde, and I was left holding Amy as she sobbed against me.

Chapter 15

Miles to go…

I will never falter, And I will not fail.

~ US Air Force Airman's Creed ~

The mood in the chopper was somber as we gained altitude. The Marines around Amy practically lifted her into the crew seat behind the co-pilot and strapped her in while the three closest to me helped me get to the tiny open spot beside her. When I knelt beside her, she pulled me to her and sobbed into my shoulder hard enough to break my heart.

"I'm sorry, Amy," I told her again and again as the Blackhawk banked to join the other helos. I didn't know if I was apologizing to her more for losing her dad or for surviving. What I did know was that there were no words that were ever going to take the pain out of this moment. Not for her, and not for me. All I could do was let her hold onto me and cry until she was done.

"Fuck!" one of the Marines yelled. "Did you see that shit!" My head came up at the fury in his voice. From where I was, I could see what he must have been talking about all too clearly through the front canopy. Ahead of us, one of engines on one of the C-130s was on fire and the other transport was falling out of the sky. The right wing of the stricken plane was already sheared off, and as it began to flip over, the left one folded up and broke away. As it spiraled down toward the ground, our chopper's pilot banked hard to the left, and a white streak zipped past our right side.

"What the fuck!" someone yelled from behind us. Amy clutched at me as the chopper came level again, and I grabbed the headset from the hook on her seat. As soon as I settled it on my head, multiple voices sounded in my ear.

"Missile's tracking!"

"Fast mover on our one o'clock!"

"I got 'im," the pilot's calmer voice came in. I looked ahead and to our right and saw the jet as it streaked toward us. At first it looked like it was heading directly at us, but when tracers drew a line ahead of it, I could see that it was aiming to our right, at one of the other Blackhawks. Sparks and holes peppered the other chopper's hull for a few seconds. It caught fire as the jet roared by, and I thought I recognized the black aircraft as an F-4 Phantom. As the other chopper went down, our pilot looked around for a moment.

"Door gunners, which way is he going?" he asked, his voice cool, almost mechanical over the headset.

"Coming around on our left side, on our left!"

"Roger that. Bobcat, Talon 3. Coming around inside the bandit's turn. Look out for him, he might try to take the shot on you." We banked right, our nose coming around deep inside the F-4's turn radius. The fighter jet hit the afterburners and almost leaped out of the way, then a missile shot out from under the broad wing and streaked toward the remaining C-130. Barely a heartbeat later, flares erupted from the C-130's fuselage, and the missile veered away from the transport's tail.

"Bandit in the kill circle," I heard the pilot say when one of the lights on the control panel went red. "Fox one, fox one." A white trail of smoke followed a silver dart from our left side and arrowed toward the black plane. In seconds it was too far away to tell if it hit or not, then the hostile jet's back end exploded and it started spinning toward the ground.

"Splash one bandit," our pilot said amid the whoops and cheers of the Marines. After a moment, the pilot spoke again. "Roger that Bobcat," he drawled. The chopper banked left.

"Alright everyone, Bobcat's picked up three more bogeys headed our way. We're gonna head for KC and try to use the smoke for cover." We gained altitude and speed, but the crippled C-130 still pulled away from us slowly. Thirty nerve-wracking minutes later, we were almost into the black curtain of smoke surrounding Kansas City. Below, I could see neighborhoods and fields on fire, with moving specks that could only be burning zombies. Then the black cloud was around us, and the smoke's acrid bite was too thick for even the Blackhawk's rotors to dispel.

With an uncharacteristic expletive, the pilot banked right, and I heard the metallic hammer of a gun behind us, even over the chopper's engine. A black chopper loomed into view in front of us, and I felt my stomach try to climb up through my throat as we shed altitude. Tracers lanced overhead, then we shot under the enemy bird and banked left, barely avoiding a line of tracer rounds that rained down on our right side. The second bandit slid into view as it banked to follow us, then it fell victim to a fatal loss of situational awareness. Tracer rounds slammed into the dark painted Blackhawk from above and to its left as our companion Blackhawk raked it with one of its miniguns.

"Sonofabitch!" someone yelled. "That was an Apache!" I felt my blood run cold at the news. I only knew of two things as tough as or tougher than an Apache gunship. One was an A-10 Thunderbolt, a tank buster of a plane known as the Warthog that sported half a ton of armor, and the 60 plus ton M1 Abrams, a main battle tank so indestructible it could withstand close range hits from its own cannons. I'd only heard of a handful of Apaches ever being shot down, and none of them had been brought down by anything short of a missile or concentrated anti-aircraft fire. The only advantage we had was that the Apache, like the Warthog and the Abrams, was designed mostly to fight targets on the ground. Of course, if it was carrying Stingers like we were, all bets were off. I looked at the lone Stinger tube on our right side and hoped it was enough.

We climbed as quickly as we could, our pilot trying to get altitude on the Apache and the still unseen third bandit. We cleared a column of thick smoke and veered right as we found the third chopper, another Blackhawk. Its pilot fired a missile the moment we saw him, but it never came close, and I didn't see the pilot's board light up to indicate the bandit had locked on to us. His door gunners were more on the ball, and opened fire on both sides as we passed. I got a brief impression of rounds hitting the left side of the chopper, then one of the Marines tackled me and shoved me back against Amy's seat. I felt impacts against the Marine on top of me, then we were through the hail of enemy fire. When he didn't move, I turned to look over my shoulder and saw a dangling eyeball and dripping gore. With a push against the seat, I shoved his body off of mine before Amy could get a good look at the ruin of his face, then turned to take stock of the situation. Blood was running across the deck, and both gunners were slumped at their guns. Looking forward I could see the pilot was dead, and the co-pilot was trying to fight the controls.

"Somebody get on one of the door guns!" the copilot was yelling over the headset. I looked back into the compartment, and only saw three Marines moving. One was pressing his hand down against his leg, the one in the middle seat against the rear wall was cradling a bloody arm, and the other was struggling to unbuckle the left door gunner's body from his seat. I turned to Amy.

"Are you hurt?" I asked her. My hands were running along her arms and legs, searching for wounds.

"No!" she yelled. "I'm okay!" I nodded to her and moved to the right door gunner's body. Trying to move a dead Marine and work the four point harness that held him in place was going to take too long. Instead, I pulled his combat knife from his belt and cut the straps, then pulled him to the side.

"Do one of you know how to use this thing?" I asked. They both nodded, then the Marine with the wounded leg pointed to the gunner's seat.

"Siddown!" he yelled. I must have looked like a fish for a moment because he yelled it at me again, this time like a drill sergeant. "It's simple! Pull the left trigger first, then the right trigger a second later. Follow your tracers and walk your fire where you want it!"

"I'm not a gunner!" I yelled at him. "I'm not even a Marine!"

"You are today!" he yelled back. I straddled the seat and grabbed the miniguns grips, looking for a target. I also tried to ignore the warm, damp feeling on my butt. As I searched, I saw black smoke coming from the engine cowling. Then the other chopper was above us and to our right. Tracer rounds sliced through the air ahead of us, and the copilot banked hard left as the deadly line of fire cut through the spot we'd just been in. When the other chopper dropped into my field of fire, I pressed the left trigger, then the right and heard the ripping sound of the minigun unleashing three thousand rounds a minute. I watched my own tracer rounds make a bright line in the air behind the other Blackhawk. I swept the spinning barrels left, then right as the bullets chewed the other helicopter's fuselage, then swept it back and forth in broad swaths to be sure I killed it.

"You're shooting at my kid!" I yelled at the black chopper as it burst into flames. I let go of the triggers and found myself breathing hard.

"Bandit left!" I heard the man on the other side yell, then the copilot brought our nose up and braked us hard in midair. Again, the metallic hammer of the Apache's thirty millimeter cannon sounded, then the other bird was passing in front of us.

The nose dropped back down, and I heard a half second of tone before the copilot called out, "Fox one, motherfucker." The Stinger pod spat its lethal payload into the air, then the rocket motor ignited and sent it straight for the Apache. The enemy pilot tried to maneuver out of the way, but we were too close for him to do more than tilt his aircraft. The missile slammed into the gunship just behind the pilot's seat, and sent the black helicopter down in a ball of fire.

"Oorah!" the Marine on the other gun called out, and the other two echoed him. I climbed over the bodies sprawled on the deck and stuck my head into the front compartment.

"How bad is it?" I asked. The copilot's face told me what I suspected, and I grabbed the pilot's headset to replace mine.

"We're gonna lose power in a couple of minutes. I can bring us in, but it ain't gonna be pretty. If we survive the landing, it might be easier than staying alive afterward."

"Am I patched into the radio on this?" I asked.

"Yes, just press that button there to transmit. Our callsign is Talon 3," he told me as he put both hands on the stick.

"Bobcat, this is Dave Stewart on Talon 3," I said, making hash of radio etiquette. Static answered me for a few seconds, then a familiar voice filled my ears.

"For Christ's sake, Stewart, you are harder to kill than a goddamn cockroach," the Marine major said with something resembling humor in his voice.

"Kind of you to say so, sir. Look, I need to ask you a favor. Is there a woman named Maya Weiss on your plane? If she is, I'd really like to talk to her."

"Is it important enough that it can't wait 'til we land, son?" he asked. Moments later, the C-130 came into sight through the smoke. "Aw, hell," I heard him say.

"I don't think we're going to be landing in the same place, so yeah, I need to know if she's still alive and if she is, I need to talk to her." Moments later, Maya's voice was in my ears, and I felt my breath catch in my throat.

"Dave? Baby, are you okay? What about Amy and Karl?" she asked. Her voice was thick with emotion, and a little rough around the edges.

"I'm fine, baby. So is Amy. Karl…he…he didn't make it. He saved our lives." I looked out the front canopy and saw the ground getting a little closer to us. I took a deep breath and steeled myself for the next part. "Look, we're going down, Maya. You're going to have to get Cassie and Bryce to Nate's. I'm sorry to put that on you, but I'm going to catch up to you as soon as I can."

"I told you not to do that to me again," she said, her tone forced.

"And I told you I couldn't promise that. But I will promise you this, Maya Weiss. Amy and I will make it back to you."

"Swear it?" her voice cracked.

"I swear it. Like I told you before, even the zombie apocalypse can't keep me away from you."

"I've got good news," she said with the barest hint of a waver in her tone. "Leo and Sherman are on the plane with us. They even got our Land Masters loaded. Did you get my care package?"

"Yeah," I said, my throat tight.

"Then you better get your ass in gear. You know how your cat gets when you're gone too long." A red light started flashing on the instrument panel, then another, and alarms started buzzing.

"I gotta go, baby. I love you," I said as the plane banked in front of us and circled to our left.

"I love you, Dave." Her voice was strong by then, and steady. I pulled the headphones off and went to the right side of the compartment. The chopper began to shudder as we got closer to the layer of smoke that blanketed the middle of Kansas City, forcing me to grab one of the straps next to the door. Then, the sound of the C-130's turboprop engines was clear and loud in my ears as it passed by on our right side. The black haze rose around us as I watched the plane head west, and we fell into darkness, the chopper's engine silent, the only thing slowing our descent the rotors themselves.

"I will never falter," I recited from the Airman's Creed as I started to strap myself into the seat beside Amy's. "And I will not fail." I reached out, grabbed her hand…and prayed.

A Letter to the Reader

Dear Reader,

Thank you for buying Zompoc: Exodus. I hope you enjoyed Dave's adventures as much as I enjoyed writing about them. Rest assured, Dave's exploits continue in Zompoc Survivor: Inferno. I'll keep you updated on the progress of the story through my website, www.chancefortunato.com, and give you glimpses into Dave's world.

Like all authors, my success depends on you, so again, I want to express my gratitude. Like most writers, I'm always trying to get better at what I do, and I'd appreciate your help with that. Please take just a few minutes to leave a review of the book and let me know what you think. Your feedback is important, and I'm glad to get it.

In the meantime, you can pick up Zompoc Survivor: Inferno to find out how Dave and Amy get out of Kansas City and learn more about the men in black and their part in the zombie apocalypse. Until then, remember the rules. Always have a Plan B.

Sincerely,
Ben Reeder

Resources:

Aside from the military hardware he picks up along the way, everything Dave uses in the story is available to buy or make. I've listed some of the places Dave would have bought his gear from below.

Zombie Tools

www.zombietools.net

These are the real life folks who made Dave's knives and sword. Great bunch of guys with a down to earth attitude. I'd trust my own life to their weapons any day.

Dark Angel Medical

http://www.darkangelmedical.com/

The folks over at Dark Angel Medical, who inspired Dave's kit in his cache tube and bug out bag. For a no-nonsense response kit, the folks at Dark Angel have you covered.

Down To Earth Foods

http://d2efoods.com/

Down To Earth Foods is the kind of place where Dave and Maya bought their bulk foods and staples, as well as their food storage containers.

Emergency Essentials

http://beprepared.com/#default

Emergency Essentials, where Dave would also have bought freeze dried foods and other essentials. Though he would have created his own bug out bags, these folks have some decent 72 hour kits of their own.

Baker Creek Heirloom Seeds

http://www.rareseeds.com/

Baker Creek Heirloom Seeds would have been Dave's choice for his seeds for the homestead. He would have gone with heirloom seeds for practical reasons, one being that they aren't dependent on any outside provider for replanting (no contracts saying you can't replant part of what you harvest, so no requirements that you buy seed from the company every year) and no dependency on certain pesticides or fertilizers for "best results."

Ruger

http://www.ruger.com/products/1022/

The Ruger 10/22 is Dave's choice of utility weapon. Light, rugged and reliable, the 10/22 is one of the most popular rifles ever made for a reason. And in spite of some of the myths out there, the .22 caliber round is perfectly capable of dropping a zombie with a head shot within 100 yards.

An excerpt from Zompoc Survivor: Inferno

Chapter 1: At Hell's Gate

I came to with the sound of gunshots and screaming in my ears. The world was a blur when I opened my eyes, but my hearing was still sharp enough to hear the tell-tale moans of infected and the sound of crazed laughter. Something moved to my right, and I swung at it. The back of my fist connected with whatever it was, and I tried to reach for it with my left hand. A band of fabric across my shoulder stopped me from moving more than a few inches, and I remembered I was strapped into a seat on a helicopter. I looked around, but my vision was still blurry. No movement on my left. Sound of something to my right. Without a thought, I reached out and grabbed at whatever was on my right. My hand fell on brittle, coarse hair; my fingers closed around it and I twisted. Something flopped on the Blackhawk's rear deck, and chilled hands grasped at my forearms. My fuzzy vision showed me a straight line, dark on one side, light on the other. My arm straightened and I tried to line up whatever was in my hand with the border of light and shadow. The shock of impact against the door frame felt good, and the dull thud of the blow was almost musical. But it was missing something, something that my brain told me I just needed to hit a little harder to hear. So I did. The second hit didn't get the job done, so I pulled my arm back a little further and slammed the thing's skull forward again. The crack of bone brought a smile to my face, and I let go of the thing in my hand. There were other things I needed to break and kill.

The pop of gunfire behind me brought my thoughts into focus, and other sounds started to make it through the haze in my head. Gunfire, voices, the groan of metal, and a moan that wasn't a zombie, all of them came clear at once. Across from me, I could see one of the Marines seated against the back of the compartment; she was turned in the seat, right hand on a bloody wound in the right leg of the Marine beside her, her left arm hanging bloody and limp at her side. On my left, Amy was slumped in her seat, and my heart froze in fear. The surviving pilot's voice, the gunfire, the other Marine's pleas to her squad mate, none of them mattered. I freed myself from the harness and dropped to one knee in front of Amy. Gently, I put my fingers under her nose and felt the slight flutter of air as she exhaled. Still breathing then. My vision seemed to be clearing slowly as I put my hand to her wrist and checked her pulse just to make sure. If she was still breathing, it made sense her heart was still beating, but I still had to check.

With Amy's safety seen to, my brain shifted gears. She was okay for the moment, but I had to make sure she stayed that way. I looked out the right side of the Blackhawk's door and saw a couple of the infected shambling across the gray surface we'd landed on. My brain replayed the last thing I remembered, the chopper not quite falling, not quite gliding toward the ground. Smoke all around us, parting at the last second to reveal a building beneath us. Then the chopper had tilted back for a moment before slamming forward hard. We were on top of a building, and there were infected on the roof. While one corner of my brain wondered why there were infected all the way up on the roof, the majority of my attention was on finding a weapon among the bodies on the blood slicked floor. I grabbed an M16 and hit the mag release. The black magazine dropped into my hand to reveal what looked like a full load. It certainly felt heavy enough. I popped it back in the well, pulled the charging handle and set the selector to single fire. I was ready to rock and roll.

"Armstrong, help me with Kale!" the wounded Marine called out as I brought the rifle up and took stock of the situation. Silence answered her. "Come on, Private! On your goddamn feet!"

"Bobcat, Talon three is down," I heard the pilot calling out from the front. "The bird is grounded, casualties unknown. We're under attack by infected." Three pops came from up front. I put my sights on one of the infected and tried to keep the red dot centered in on its face when I pulled the trigger. The gun bucked against my shoulder, but the zombie's head stayed intact. I fired twice more before I put a round through its left eye. I swung the gun to my right and found the other one. It went down on the second try, and I counted off five rounds. I glanced through the cockpit and saw several more coming toward us.

From the rear compartment I couldn't get a good shot at them, so I hopped to the ground. The world tilted under my feet and I stumbled a couple of steps before I got my balance back. As close as these four were, it was easier to get a shot at their faces. It only took me ten shots to get four rounds into their skulls. A quick look at the far side of the chopper and to the rear showed me no infected, though the incessant moaning was still reaching my ears. I turned my head to follow the sound and nearly dropped the gun.

The building we'd landed on had another section butted up against it and a structure on the roof. It was hard to tell directions in the heavy smoke over the city, but the chopper's nose was pointed diagonally across the roof, and the small structure was almost right in front of its nose on the opposite side. The infected I'd just shot had been near it. Off to my right across the roof was an unfinished looking section, and it was absolutely thick with infected, at least fifty if I had to guess. My slowly clearing vision also caught something else: several bodies between the unfinished section and the chopper. People I knew I hadn't shot. The mysterious dead people could wait, though. I figured they'd stay dead for a little while longer, but unless I did something *fast,* odds were stacking up in favor of me being just as dead for just as long. Short of a bomb, there was no way I was going to kill that many infected with an assault rifle before they got to us. I couldn't get that many rounds downrange in time.

An inhuman scream cut off my frantic search for options, and I looked back toward the unfinished section. Every one of the dead infected was looking my way now as another one, a ghoul in blue-green scrubs opened her mouth and let out another scream from the edge of the roof. The dead infected behind her started shuffling toward us like they had a purpose the second her voice ripped across my eardrums. The rifle was up to my shoulder before I could even think about it, and I put round after round into her torso. Her body jerked with the impact of each bullet, and I walked my rounds up her body until I was putting shots center mass. Finally, she fell to her knees, and I brought the red sight on her nose.

"Die, motherfucker," I snarled as I pulled the trigger. The moment her head jerked back, the zombies stopped moving toward us for a moment, and I felt a brief sense of accomplishment. Then their collective gaze zeroed in on the chopper again, and desperation gave birth to a solution. What I needed was a way to put a lot of bullets into a lot of zombies in a very short time, and I had just the gun for that.

Buy Zompoc Survivor: Inferno on Amazon.

From The Paean of Sundered Dreams!

At the end of the world, one woman holds the only key to the future, written in madness and blood.

Fifteen years after the events in *Rationality Zero*, Earth falls to an apocalypse that none could have seen. In this whisper of a possible future, the worst nightmare of the Facility comes into being.

But is it true? Or are we simply peering into the mind of a deranged woman, who cannot tell fact from fiction?

In this odd story, which nestles uncomfortably into the timelines of ***Rationality Zero, The Herald of Autumn, Collateral Damage***, and ***The Primary Protocol***, Rational Earth falls to the darkness of the Shroud. Will our world recover from the desolation of darkness and madness that storms at the center of creation? Or, like the world of **Cæstre**, will all that man has wrought be lost?

None can say. Whether terrifying truth or irrational fantasy, one young woman holds the fate of all in her trembling hands.

What are people saying about "The Wormwood Event?"

One of the better short stories I've read in a while. Great flow throughout the story. I will definitely read more of this author.

This is a real chiller-thriller book. While you're trying to contain your shivers, your heart is thumping with the excitement of what's going to happen next.

This was my first time stepping into a world brought to life by JM Guillen and I am still in awe of his words.

This was my first experience of this author and I highly recommend him based on what I've seen so far.

First in the Paean of Sundered Dreams!

The world is not what it seems.

Michael Bishop has is an Asset of the Facility—a job that comes with many strange perks. He is a man who never gets ill, who never pays taxes. He is effortlessly fit, and has a different woman every night of the week.

That is, when he is not on assignment.

When activated, Michael becomes Asset 108, an enhanced human who stands against the strange darkness that lurks at the edge of our world.

Armed with equipment that most would find impossible to comprehend, he is sent on missions both strange and deadly. Each dossier pits him against irrational creatures and beings—most with the power to unravel his sanity, or reality itself.

It's never a simple job.

This one, however, is more complex than most. Mysterious unknown targets are fracturing reality, somewhere in the middle of the Mojave Desert.

The Facility has no other Assets in the area, and their telemetry is spotty at best. Without knowing what to expect, Bishop is activated, assigned to a cadre, and sent to the middle of nowhere.

What he finds there is both the beginning and the end.

Made in the USA
San Bernardino, CA
16 January 2017